Dear Reader,

I can hardly believe that it is almost twenty years since I wrote my first Harlequin book. The thrill of having that book accepted and then seeing it on the bookshelves—being picked up and chosen by readers—is one I shall never forget.

Twenty years seems a long time. So much has happened during those years; so much has changed and yet so much remains the same. The changes that we have all seen within society are, I believe, reflected in the books we, as Harlequin authors, write. They mirror the changes that take place around us in our own and our readers' lives. Our heroines have changed, matured, grown up, as indeed I have done myself. I cannot tell you how much pleasure it gives me to be able to write of mature—as well as young— women finding love. And, of course, love is something that has not changed. Love is still love and always will be, because love is, after all, an intrinsic, vital component of human happiness.

As I read through these books that are being reissued in this Collector's Edition, they bring back for me many happy memories of the times when I wrote them, and I hope that my readers, too, will enjoy the same nostalgia and pleasure.

I wish you all very many hours of happy reading and lives blessed with love.

Penny Jordan

Back by Popular Demand

Penny Jordan is one of the world's best loved as well as bestselling authors, and she was first published by Harlequin in 1981. The novel that launched her career was *Falcon's Prey,* and since then she has gone on to write more than one hundred books. In this special collection, Harlequin is proud to bring back a selection of these highly sought after novels. With beautiful cover art created by artist Erica Just, this is a Collector's Edition to cherish.

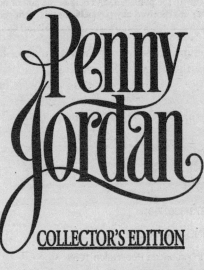

Penny Jordan

COLLECTOR'S EDITION

Levelling the Score

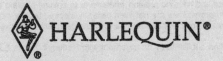

HARLEQUIN®

TORONTO • NEW YORK • LONDON
AMSTERDAM • PARIS • SYDNEY • HAMBURG
STOCKHOLM • ATHENS • TOKYO • MILAN • MADRID
PRAGUE • WARSAW • BUDAPEST • AUCKLAND

ISBN 0-373-63077-8

LEVELLING THE SCORE

First North American Publication 1988.

ERICA JUST
cover illustrator for the
Penny Jordan Collector's Edition

Erica Just is an artist and illustrator working in various media, including watercolor, pen and ink, and textiles. Her studio is in Nottingham, England.

Her work is inspired by the natural forms, architecture and vibrant colors that she has experienced on her travels, most especially in Africa and India.

Erica has exhibited her work extensively in Great Britain and Europe and has works in private and public collections. As an illustrator she works for a number of companies and also lectures on textile design throughout the country.

CHAPTER ONE

'JENNA, *please*...you've got to help me, there just isn't anyone else. God, if only I'd listened to you years ago... You warned me what sort of brother I've got, but—'

'Susie, come on, you're exaggerating,' Jenna interrupted her volatile friend. 'Simon can't stop you from marrying whoever you wish—nor force you into marrying someone against your will. You're twenty-four, for God's sake, and he *is* only your elder brother...'

'He's no brother of mine. Not any more,' Susie responded theatrically. 'Machiavelli would be a better name for him. God, to think I never guessed what he was up to, all the time he was shovelling that gross friend of his down my throat...go to the theatre... All the time I thought I was doing it to help Simon out with an old friend suffering from loneliness, and now I find out that Simon has been trying to marry me off to the guy.'

'What's he like?' Jenna asked curiously.

Susie frowned, her blonde hair with its soft pink streaks standing up on end all round her small head. No matter how outlandish her clothes and hair-style might be, there was an unmistakable soft femininity about Susie that simply couldn't be hidden. She had been having man trouble of one sort or another for as long as Jenna had known her, and that had been since they had both started senior school together when they were eleven years old.

'Who, Simon? Come on, it isn't that long since you last saw him... My twenty-first, wasn't it? And he hasn't changed that much... Men don't, do they, not once they get over thirty... He still looks deliciously distinguished...especially when he's wearing his court gear. He hasn't gone grey, though, or anything like that. Odd, isn't it, that he should have such dark hair, black as a crow's wing really, and mine should be so fair... Ma reckons he inherited his colouring from a Cornish great-grandmother...'

Jenna subdued a faint sigh at her friend's ramblings, and then interrupted firmly, 'No, Susie, not Simon! What's his friend like, the one he wants you to marry?'

'You mean you *will* help me? Oh, my God, Jenna, I knew you would! I know it will work, the minute he sets eyes on you he's bound to fall for you... It's not fair...why couldn't I be tall and slim, instead of small and round? And your hair, I've always yearned for dark red hair...it's so...so...'

'Red?' Jenna supplied challengingly, with a gleam in her eyes, quite forgetting for the moment that as yet she had most definitely not made any commitment to help her friend rid herself of her unwanted suitor, no matter what Susie might choose to believe.

Her red hair was a constant source of irritation to her. People who didn't know her constantly made reference to the temper they suspected must go with it. Others, normally women, asked her if it was dyed... It *was* a rather spectacular shade of dense, dark red. It went well with her creamy skin, although untypically her eyes were not gold or green, but a dark, true sapphire-blue.

All her life she had had pinned on her the label of a redhead's infamous temper, and because of it she had cultivated a cool remoteness that outwardly at least she allowed nothing to shake.

The temper was there all right, but she hated being predictable. And if there was one person above all others who had the knack of arousing that temper it was Simon Townsend.

They had first met when she was twelve and he was nineteen. Susie had taken her home with her after school. An only child herself, she had been inclined to stand in awe of the elder brother Susie talked so much about, even before she had met him.

It had a been a summer's afternoon, and they had arrived from school, hot and sticky. Simon, home from university, had been playing tennis, but he had come in looking cool and unflappable in his tennis whites, his dark hair slicked smoothly to his masculine skull, his eyes cool and unfathomable, making Jenna feel as though he was looking right into her mind and reading every single little thing that was hidden there.

So powerful was the memory of that meeting that she actually squirmed uncomfortably in her chair.

Susie, at last realising the whole of her best friend's attention was not focused upon her, broke off in mid-sentence and stared at her, her brown eyes rounded and filling with tears.

'Jenna, please...*please* help me. You don't know what it's like to be in love, the way Peter and I are...'

'No, I don't,' Jenna agreed firmly. 'Nor can I see why you don't simply tell dear brother Simon to forget his empire-building plans and say you're in love with someone else! Come on, Susie, he can't force you into marriage with this friend of his... Your parents wouldn't let him.'

'You don't know Simon,' Susie responded darkly. 'It's becoming a barrister that's done it—all that power, it's gone to his head. You *know* how persuasive he can be, Jenna, once he starts talking to me...' She gave a tiny, but effective shiver, making Jenna remember rather wryly the fact that she had been one of the leading lights in their theatrical group when they were at school.

'It's all right for you,' Susie continued miserably. 'You're so strong-willed, so firm in what you want to do. I'm not, and once Simon gets to work on me, I'm terrified that he'll get me to agree to doing something I don't really want to do... The problem is that he detests poor Peter, even though he's only met him once... And just because Peter forgot to put his hand-brake on and ran into the back of Simon's car... Such a fuss about a piece of tin! Of course, that made Simon take against him right from the start, but I didn't realise then just what he'd got in mind for me. Ma let it drop the other weekend when I went to see them. I told her that Peter and I were planning to go away on holiday together this year, and Ma said that she thought I would have been going to Canada with John... She got all flustered and het up about it, so I guessed there was something going on, and I got her to admit to me that Simon thinks I should marry John...'

'I still can't see why you need my help.'

'You know me, I'm hopeless at confrontation scenes. You know how weak I am.'

Visions of the many disappointed young men she had had to send away from their front door in the days when they had shared university digs together came to Jenna's mind...

'Please, Jen! All I'm asking you to do is to cover for me while Peter and I go away... We need time to be alone...time together without Simon interfering. We're going down to Cornwall. The folks still have the house down there... Remember it?'

Jenna did. Many years ago when she and Susie had both been in their early teens, she, and her grand-mother who had brought her up after her parents' death in an avalanche while they were on a skiing holiday, had spent several happy summer holidays with Susie and her parents at their holiday home in Cornwall, holidays made all the more pleasant because Simon had not shared them—he had been away at university, and then later undertaking his training for the bar.

It was a long time since she and Susie had holidayed together; the last time had been the summer they had left university, when they had travelled all through Europe together. On that occasion, too, she remembered Simon raising objections about their plans. Her mouth compressed slightly as she remembered this and other things...

Simon Townsend could sometimes be too sure of himself and the rightness of his own judgement for his own good. She had few fears that scatty, pretty Susie could ever be inveigled into marriage with anyone—she liked to play the field—but Susie was right about one thing. Simon was a very effective verbal opponent, and Susie, who disliked any kind of conversation that did not focus around fashion, was all too likely to give in to him, simply to keep him quiet.

'What exactly is it you want me to do?' she asked, disentangling herself from Susie's fiercely jubilant hug.

'I'm going to tell Simon that I'm staying here with you... He's bound to ring you to check up on me. All I want you to do is to confirm that I'm here!'

'And if my verbal confirmation isn't enough?' Jenna pressed.

It took Susie several seconds to work it out. 'Oh,

you mean if he wants to speak to me?' A grin curled her mouth. 'I've thought of the most delicious plan. It will completely fool him... I've made a tape.'

She delved into her huge shoulder-bag and fished out a small recorder complete with tape. 'Look, I'll play it for you. You pretend to be Simon, and then listen...'

Dutifully, Jenna did as she was instructed. When the tape ended she surveyed her friend with mixed feelings and a certain amount of wry resignation.

The tape was an ingenious idea, and Susie knew her brother well enough to be able to anticipate what line his conversation would take. The answers she had dictated on to the tape were vague and Susie-ish enough to be quite convincing.

'See, you'll have no problems,' Susie told her proudly, pressing a button to rewind the machine. 'I've thought of everything!'

'Including Simon descending on me in person?' Jenna asked drily.

'Oh, he won't do that, he'll be on circuit. You know, travelling with the judges and things...how they do. He won't be back in London for simply ages, and I'll be back myself then...'

'You're sure this is only a holiday you and Peter are going on? You're not running away to get married or anything like that, are you?' Jenna demanded ominously.

'Of course not! You know me, I don't want to get married for ages yet.'

Jenna knew when Susie was telling the truth.

'No, I just want time to get to know him properly, Jenna, without Simon popping up all the time and spoiling things. You wouldn't believe what he's been like these last few weeks… I think he must be watching my flat, because the moment Peter comes round, Simon arrives. I'm twenty-four years old, and I've got big brother watching over me as though I was a child. It's ridiculous,' Susie fumed, 'especially when you think of the girlfriends Simon's had. He hasn't exactly lived like a monk,' she finished darkly.

Jenna didn't try to argue with her. Only the other day, there had been a rather spectacular exposé of the latest bright star on the legal world's horizon's involvement with the ex-wife of a government minister.

For intensely personal and private reasons Jenna had studied the article closely and the photographs that went with it.

She hadn't needed her friend's rambling description of the lack of changes in her brother's appearance to know what Simon looked like. Susie had been right, the dark hair was untouched by grey, the firm mouth with its curving, full underlip still curled in the same mocking smile, and his eyes…those chameleon, challenging green eyes that should have belonged to her, still carried their same message of chilly warning.

The woman photographed with him had been like all the other women who had passed through Simon's life; blonde, *soignée*, sophisticated and very, very beautiful.

Would he marry this one? The gossip press seemed to think so. It wasn't like the high and mighty Simon to marry someone else's cast-off, she thought acidly. If she pictured him with a wife at all, it was with someone young and malleable, someone he could mould to his own desired pattern of what a wife should be.

'What's wrong?' Susie demanded, adding succinctly, 'Your eyes have gone almost black, they only do that when you're fuming with someone. Anyone I know?'

When Jenna shook her head, Susie heaved a faint sigh.

'There must be something wrong with you, Jen,' she accused. 'Look at you, you're the most gorgeous-looking creature,' she said generously. 'Men buzz round you like bees round honey, and yet you ignore them all. When we were kids, I always thought you'd be the one who grew up and got married young...'

'When exactly is it that you're supposed to be going off on this holiday of yours?' Jenna asked, ruthlessly cutting through her friend's reminiscences.

'Today! This afternoon... God, I wish I could see Simon's face if he discovers the bird's flown,' she said with a chuckle.

'Don't laugh too soon,' Jenna advised her darkly. 'It can always be arranged...'

'You won't betray me, Jen. I know that... Once Simon—'

'I can't see why you simply don't tell Simon what you're doing.'

'Because if I do, he'll try to dissuade me. You know what he's like.' Susie gave a heartfelt groan. 'The problem is, I'm so used to doing what he tells me that I'm frightened I'll go on doing it, even when it isn't what I want... Simon can be so—so compelling at times.'

'Hero-worship,' Jenna scoffed. 'You should have grown out of that years ago.'

'You don't know how lucky you are not to have any brothers or sisters. Just you and your grandmother, and she'd never force you into doing anything you don't want to do.'

Jenna could have pointed out to her that there were methods of enforcing one's wishes other than those adopted by Susie's elder brother, but she refrained, sensing that Susie would never understand the gentle, tender pressure one old lady with a longing to see her one grandchild 'settled down', as she called it, could bring to bear on that same grandchild.

Long after Susie had gone, blowing her a string of kisses and promising to get in touch, Jenna remained sitting in her armchair.

Her flat was small and pin-neat, furnished by 'bargains' she had acquired through her job as personal assistant to a very dynamic and go-ahead interior designer.

If she had had any sense, any sense at all, she would have refused to help Susie. Simon Townsend could be a very powerful adversary indeed, as she already had good cause to know. She closed her eyes and lay back in the comfortable chair.

The summer she had been fifteen, she had fallen madly and very obviously in love with Simon Townsend, but it had very plainly been made clear just how impossible were the foolish dreams she had been dreaming...

Her adolescent crush on him had faded as adolescent crushes do, but it had left behind a sense of bitterness and resentment, and antagonism towards him that Jenna had never lost, and which had made her weary and cautious in all her dealings with his sex.

In her heart of hearts she suspected that she had agreed to help Susie in her crazy plan because she would enjoy the opportunity of thwarting Simon.

For all her dizziness, Susie could be extremely astute. If she said that her brother was trying to foist one of his friends off on her, then she was probably quite right. Simon had always had a decided inclination to meddle in the affairs of others, an irritating 'I know best' attitude it would give her a great deal of pleasure to squash.

This time he wouldn't be dealing with an immature, gauche fifteen-year-old, but a woman of twenty-four, well able to use the brain God had given her, and not afraid of meeting any man on equal terms.

The phone call which had preceded Susie's early morning Saturday visit had disrupted her entire day. She had planned to go home and see her grandmother, but now it was too late.

The Gloucestershire village where Susie's parents and Jenna's grandmother lived was a quiet, remote place, but she often missed it. Susie had been right when she claimed that she had always imagined that Jenna would settle down first.

As a teenager, she had wanted nothing more than to fall in love, marry and raise a family in the familiar environment of the village. But teenagers grew up, and now the idea of marriage had lost a good deal of its lustre.

She had seen too many of her friends' marriages dissolve under the pressure of modern-day living, and had grown to cherish her single state. No one in her wide circles of friends knew of the money she was carefully hoarding away, against the day when she could fulfil at least a part of her teenage dream.

When she had saved enough it was her ambition to return home; to buy herself a small cottage close to her grandmother's, and start up her own business, offering a combination of services for which she knew there was a need, such as house-and pet-sitting, book-keeping and typing, gardening and cleaning.

It was her ambition to build up a private agency that would provide all of these services and more, and she was convinced that she could do it, once she had enough capital behind her.

Not even Susie knew what she was planning. To Susie her dreams would be mundane, boring even; Susie loved the bright lights of London, the glamour of the fashion world in which she moved. As an assistant director on a glossy magazine, she lived every minute of her life to the full and wouldn't be able to understand Jenna's desire to return home.

Her flat was on the ground floor of a small terraced house which belonged to a friend—a photographer who travelled a lot, and who was only too relieved to have a tenant as careful and reliable as Jenna.

The house possessed a small backyard, which she had transformed with several coats of white paint and a collection of terracotta pots and trellising, holding up a collection of climbing plants. She spent most of the afternoon pottering around in it, enjoying the warmth of the early summer's day.

Craig was due back tomorrow. He had been working in the Seychelles on a fashion feature for Susie's magazine.

A charismatic, sometimes moody man in his late thirties, he was involved in what seemed to Jenna to be a hopeless relationship with a married woman who was tied to a physically handicapped husband. But then, who was she to criticise other people's relationships, she asked herself with a graceful shrug, when she deliberately held herself back from any form of emotional commitment?

Was it prudence that made her so cautious, or was it fear? She pushed the thought aside, not wanting to give in to the mood of introspection slowly enveloping her.

Crossly she blamed Simon Townsend for her unwanted thoughts. He had always had a disturbing effect on her, and apparently it hadn't lessened.

If she had been so inclined, she could have been wryly amused by Susie's defection. Her friend had played the doting sister for so long that Jenna had long ago given up trying to make her see that her adored brother was only a man.

On her way round the pretty town garden, she did pause to wonder how Simon himself would react to Susie's rebellion. His opinions had held sway with his younger sister for so long, it would probably come as an almighty shock.

Susie's parents, although darlings, were almost as much in awe of their elder child as Susie herself.

His father was a placid, kindly man, now retired, who had once taught at a local public school. His mother was the stronger character of the two, but without the bruising acidity of her eldest child.

As a teenager, still raw from the loss of her own parents, Jenna had grown to look on Susie's mother and father as sort of adopted parents, just as Susie had come to look on Jenna's grandmother as a member of *her* family.

A cool breeze sprang up, bringing goose-bumps to her arms. She went inside, showered and changed out of her jeans and T-shirt into a silky wraparound dress that emphasised the softness of her curves. Her hair hung down on to her shoulders, curling softly, her face—without make-up—oddly young and vulnerable. As she walked through her small sitting-room her eyes fell to the small tape recorder on the table beside the phone.

Well, Susie had made her escape. It just remained now for her to convince Simon that his sister was safely ensconced with her.

She was just about to start making her own early evening meal, when she remembered that she had promised to stock up Craig's fridge. Susie's visit had completely banished her promise from her mind. She glanced at her watch, and breathed a faint sigh of relief. There was still time to get what she needed from the shops.

A row of lock-up garages to the rear of the garden held her small Mini. She drove it with the same care and caution she applied to everything else.

Craig was a lazy cook, and so she stocked up on pizza, and a selection of cold meats and other delicacies from his favourite delicatessen.

If he followed his normal routine, the moment he returned he would head for his darkroom, where he would develop the prints he had taken on location, and he would only emerge once he had finished working, whatever time of the night or day that might be.

There was no sign of him when she got back and, using the key he had given her, she went up to his flat and put away her purchases, pausing to open the windows to let in some fresh air before going back down to her own domain.

The phone was ringing as she walked in, and she picked it up without thinking, half anticipating hearing Craig's voice announcing that he was at the airport and on his way back.

Instead, Simon's crisp, authoritative voice assaulted her unprepared ear-drum, her whole body tensing as she gripped the receiver.

'Jenna, I understand Susie's staying with you?'

'Yes...yes, she is...'

'Could I have a word with her?'

She stared blankly at the cream-painted wall of her sitting-room, and then thankfully remembered Susie's tape.

'Yes... Yes, I'll just go and get her.'

She fumbled with the 'on' switch of the tape, and accidentally knocked it to the floor. When she picked it up the tape was running, but no sound was emerging. She stared at it in horror. Something had gone wrong!

She trembled as she picked up the tape machine, the fact that Simon was still waiting to speak to Susie forgotten as, to her horror, she saw that the 'erase' button of the tape was depressed.

How had it happened? A fluke of mischance, catching it as it had fallen? Or had Susie—scatty, lovable, Susie—depressed it by mistake?

She would never know; what she *did* know was

that Simon was going to be unable to speak to his sister.

She picked up the receiver and took a deep breath, forcing her voice to sound as light and careless as possible as she said calmly. 'Simon, I'm sorry. I've just been out to the shops... Susie's in the bath and apparently likely to be there for some time. She says she'll ring you later...' She crossed her fingers childishly and added, 'Are you going out this evening, or...?'

She was taking a chance on the fact that since it was a Saturday evening Simon was sure to be going out somewhere or other with his new lover.

There was a pause, and then when he spoke there was a certain unnerving grimness about Simon's voice as he responded curtly, 'Yes...yes, as a matter of fact, I shall be going out.'

He rang off before she could say anything else, leaving her feeling idiotically shaken and extremely unnerved.

What was the matter with her? He was only a man, as she had so often remarked to her friend. She must be getting as soft as Susie to let him get to her like this.

Ah well, it was over now. Simon had quite obviously accepted the fact that Susie was staying with her, and her friend had no doubt made good her escape with the unfortunate Peter, of whom Simon appeared to disapprove so heartily.

She could relax and put the Townsend family

firmly out of her mind. She had no plans for the evening; there were friends she could have gone out with, but it had been a hectic week with her boss returning from a week in the South of France, where he had been supervising the final details of a property he had been commissioned to work on. And on his return a dozen or more impatient clients had been waiting to see him.

She was suffering from the pleasurable tiredness that came from having worked hard, both physically and mentally, and she was looking forward to a lazy evening with a tray of tempting nibbles, a pot of strong coffee and the latest Sidney Sheldon to keep her company.

CHAPTER TWO

JENNA had just reached the part where the story was starting to develop properly when her doorbell rang. She groaned, putting her book down reluctantly. It would be Craig, too lazy to search for his own key again.

She got up and went to open the door.

'Hello, Jenna. I trust my sister is now *out* of the bath?'

As she fought to control her shock, her attention slid past Simon's tall, laconic figure to the car parked just behind him. Good heavens, if that was Simon's, no wonder he had objected to Susie's new love running into the back of it! She blinked slightly as she took in the luxurious splendour of its dark maroon paintwork.

'It's an Aston Martin,' he told her helpfully, following her gaze. 'The soft top signifies that it's a convertible.'

The sarcasm underlying his words snapped her back to reality. This was the Simon she knew so well.

'I *can* see that for myself.'

'You can? You surprise me, Jenna!'

What was he implying? She shifted uneasily from

one foot to the other, not having the courage to ask. If she did, no doubt she would receive another sardonic insult.

'Aren't you going to invite me in?'

She didn't want to. Had he already guessed the truth, or was he genuinely expecting to find Susie inside her flat?

The sudden screech of a taxi as it came to a halt inches from the Aston Martin's immaculate bodywork created a welcome diversion.

The door opened and Craig emerged, looking very brown and slightly leaner than Jenna remembered.

He paid off the taxi, and gathered up his belongings.

'Hi, gorgeous... Missed me?' he asked, ignoring Simon to plant a warm kiss very firmly against Jenna's mouth.

His action took her by surprise. An easy camaraderie existed between her and Craig but, while he would often slip his arm round her, or tease her about her non-existent sex life, this was the first time he had actually kissed her.

'I hope you've got something in for supper, I'm starving...'

'I filled your fridge for you,' Jenna told him automatically, her attention focused on Simon, and on the extraordinary tension that was emanating from him. What was causing it? The fact that she was keeping him waiting on the doorstep? And yet he hadn't seemed all that anxious when he'd first asked for Susie.

'Lend me your key will you, Jen?' Craig asked. 'God knows where mine is.'

She stepped back into the hallway automatically in response to his request, both men following her. When she emerged into the light of the sitting-room she saw that the tension had left Simon's face, and that he was his usual urbane, relaxed self.

'Know you from somewhere, don't I?' Craig asked Simon, while Jenna got her spare key to his flat.

'Not as far as I'm aware.'

The silky denial irritated Jenna for some reason.

'You've probably seen his picture in the gossip columns,' she told Craig, eyeing Simon with disfavour.

'Really?' Craig looked curious, but not impressed.

'Are you going to come up and have supper with me later, Jen?' Craig asked. 'Or...'

'Jenna and I have some personal family business to discuss,' Simon answered smoothly for her. 'Private family business...'

Craig took the hint, the look he gave Jenna over Simon's shoulder as he opened the door to leave making her expel a faint shaky sigh of relief.

It was good to know that Craig would be upstairs if she needed him, although quite what Simon could do if he discovered that Susie had deceived him she wasn't too sure.

'Er…would you like a cup of coffee, Simon, or…?'

'What I would like, Jenna, is to know exactly what game my idiotic sister is playing now. And don't try telling me that she's staying here with you.' His eyes swept the neatness of the small room disparagingly. 'I know my sister…if she were here, there's no way she wouldn't already have littered the place with her possessions.'

Jenna bit down on her bottom lip, knowing that what he said was all too true.

'Where is she, Jenna?'

The silkiness was gone from his voice now, leaving it hard and determined. He must be a very frightening man to face in court, she thought on a soft shiver.

'Susie is twenty-four-years old, Simon,' she told him, stalling for time. 'If she wanted you to know her every movement, I'm sure she'd let you know…'

'Nice try, but it won't wash… Susie is up to something, probably with that moronic idiot, Halbury!'

'Susie loves him,' Jenna retorted angrily.

'So she *is* with him!' Triumph glinted darkly in his eyes. 'I thought as much, the stupid little fool… If she can't see that it's her trust fund he's in love with…'

'You've no right to say that,' Jenna interrupted him.

'Haven't I? Have you met Halbury yet, Jenna?'

She bit her lips again, in vexed admission that he had caught her out.

'You know my sister… How many times has she been in love in the last five or six years? Once a month on average, wouldn't you say?'

Jenna was forced to concede that he had a point, but she conceded it in silence.

'The man's nothing more than a fortune-hunter,' Simon told her bitterly. 'He's filled Susie's head with some idiotic idea that he's a talented fashion designer, and that with her money…'

'Maybe he's right,' Jenna suggested tartly. 'Just because the all-seeing, all-knowing Simon Townsend doesn't approve of him, doesn't necessarily mean…'

'All right, Jenna, you can cut out the acid remarks. He's been made bankrupt twice in the last four years. Before he started dating Susie he was involved with the eighteen-year-old daughter of a building millionaire, but Daddy realised what was going on and put a stop to it. Halbury must have thought he'd strayed into paradise when he found Susie.'

His voice held such a ring of bitterness, that Jenna went cold with anxiety for her friend. It was true that Susie was not and never had been a good judge of character. She took everyone at face value, believing that all her fellow human beings were as honest and innocent as she herself.

Because the Townsend family as a whole played down the money inherited from a wealthy industrialist uncle of their father's, Jenna herself had almost forgotten about it. Now her forehead pleated with concern, as she said slowly, 'But surely Susie can't touch her trust fund until she's thirty?'

'Or marries beforehand, in which case she inherits when she's twenty-five—in four months' time,' Simon reminded her.

Immediately Jenna felt herself flush with guilt. She ought to have questioned Susie more deeply, knowing her feather-headed friend's prosperity for trouble, but she had been so caught up in the potential pleasure of putting Simon's nose out of joint that she had completely overlooked this facet of Susie's personality.

Another unpalatable thought struck her. Had Susie, knowing how she felt about Simon, deliberately introduced him into the situation as a ploy—a decoy, so that she wouldn't question her too deeply? And then she remembered the rest of what Susie had told her.

'Susie's old enough to make up her own mind about whom she wants to marry, Simon,' she told him. 'Since you know your sister so well, I'm surprised that you didn't realise what the effect of trying to force her hand would be,' she concluded, with an admirable attempt to mimic his own sardonic coolness.

'Ah, I see… So now I'm featuring as the big bad brother, am I? I take it that Susie has been discussing John Cameron with you?'

'She told me that you were trying to coerce her

into marrying one of your friends—yes,' Jenna
agreed baldly.

His eyebrows rose mockingly. 'Is that really what
she told you? Goodness me, she must have a more
inventive imagination than I'd given her credit for.
And you believed her?'

His smile wasn't kind, and it raised an anguished
pattern of goose-bumps down the length of her spine.

'Do tell me, Jenna—how was the dastardly deed
to be accomplished? Was I going to drug her and
carry her off somewhere, where I could keep her imprisoned until she agreed to marry John, or...'

'Don't be so ridiculous!' Jenna snapped, interrupting him, bright flags of colour flying in her
cheeks. 'I know what you're trying to do, Simon, but
it won't work. I know you, remember...there are far
more subtle ways of bringing force to bear on someone. Susie was afraid that she would let you persuade
her into marriage with this—this John...'

'Umm...I suppose she neglected to mention that
less than twelve months ago when she first met him
in Canada, she was actually engaged to John, albeit
very fleetingly. She broke off the engagement when
he told her that they would be living on his money.'

Jenna felt herself flush again. She wasn't' sure
whom she was the most annoyed with, Susie, Simon,
or herself for being such a gullible idiot.

'Where have they gone, Jenna? And don't bother
trying to lie to me. I know she's gone off somewhere
with this Halbury idiot.'

'Cornwall,' Jenna told him, defeated. 'Your parents' house... She wanted time on her own with him, to get to know him properly...'

Defeat and guilt tasted acid in her mouth. Simon was just as capable of shading the truth as Susie herself, but in this instance... She gnawed on her bottom lip, wishing she had never got involved in the situation in the first place.

'What are you going to do?'

'What do you think?' Simon asked ironically.

'Go down and bring her back?'

'Clever girl!' He glanced at his watch, revealing a tanned forearm, crisped with very masculine-looking dark hairs.

'Enjoyable though I find your company, Jenna, I'm afraid I've got to go...'

'Will you drive down there tonight?'

He raised his eyebrows slightly.

'Like a knight on a white charger, intent on protecting my sister's virtue?' He shook his head. 'No, not tonight.' He walked to the door, and then paused, turning to eye her thoughtfully. 'By the way, do give my apologies to your...friend, for interrupting his... homecoming...'

Jenna caught the underlying message and gritted her teeth against it. 'There's no need to be coy, Simon,' she responded coolly. 'If you're trying to intimate that you believe Craig and I are lovers, why not come right out and say so? After all, there isn't any reason why we shouldn't be, is there?'

'None,' he agreed cordially, giving her a hard-edged look. 'And although it's none of my business, I have to say that you hardly took the part of the eager lover, desperate to return to his arms,' he told her with gentle malice.

She couldn't let it pass, it came too close to home, too close to a truth she couldn't bear to admit.

'Craig and I have lived together for quite a long time, Simon,' she responded calmly. 'Neither of us seems to need the constant stimulation of new partners... But then we're all of us different, aren't we?' she added with an acid smile.

If her barb had found its mark, there was no sign of it. She followed Simon out into the hall, and let him out of the front door. She watched as he walked away, a tall man, who, despite being powerfully built, moved with a lithe grace that could on occasion be faintly menacing.

When he had gone she went back to her sitting-room, her interest in her book now completely gone. She had failed Susie; now what was she to do?

She looked at the phone and then remembered that the house in Cornwall did not possess one. It was a holiday home, Mrs Townsend had always said, and that being the case, a telephone could only be an unwanted intrusion.

She thought of Susie, still blissfully unaware of what tomorrow would bring. Her friend had quite probably deliberately deceived her. Simon might be correct in everything he had said about Peter Halbury, but that did not alter the fact that he still had no right to interfere in his sister's life, Jenna told herself stubbornly.

Somehow Susie would have to be warned. But how?

There *was* only one way, and she knew even as she contemplated it that her mind was already made up, and had been from the moment Simon had announced that he wouldn't be going to Cornwall until the morning.

It would be a long drive, and an uncomfortable one in her small Mini, but the very thought of depriving Simon of his prey was enough to make her ignore any potential discomfort.

She went upstairs to Craig's flat. He opened the door immediately to her knock.

'Gone, then, has he?' He looked speculatively at her, but Jenna refused to be drawn.

'Yes, he has. Craig, I have to go down to Cornwall—immediately... Will you keep an eye on my flat? I'll only be gone for a couple of days.'

She sensed that Craig wanted to question her, but after a moment's hesitation he shrugged and said laconically, 'Of course, why not? You're not thinking of taking that car of yours, I hope?'

'What else?'

'Take mine instead,' he offered.

Craig owned a six-month-old Porsche that was his joy and pride, and Jenna blinked slightly at the munificence of this offer.

'Craig, I couldn't!'

'Of course you could. You'll be a damn sight safer driving mine than that tin can of yours.'

Reluctantly she allowed him to persuade her, knowing that the journey would be faster and much easier in Craig's car.

He gave her the keys, and she went back down to her own flat to pack an overnight case.

Within an hour she was on the road, busy with mid-evening traffic, but once she had cleared the city she had the motorway almost to herself. The Porsche was a dream to drive, eating up the miles. The route was familiar to her from all the holidays she had shared with Susie and her family at their Cornish cottage, and although she had to stop three or four times to check signposts, once she was off the motorway she felt that she was making good time.

Susie would be shocked to see her, but better that shock than the one she would get should Simon turn up unannounced some time tomorrow afternoon.

At last she was crossing the Tamar—always an important psychological moment in those teenage journeys—and finally she was on Cornish land.

Although both Susie and Simon shared their Cornish ancestry, only Simon showed it, with his olive skin and night-dark hair. Mrs Townsend had once voiced the opinion that she suspected there might even be a trace of Spanish blood somewhere in their Cornish inheritance—Spanish galleons had been wrecked off the Cornish coast at the time of the ill-fated Armada, and more than one dark-haired, swarthy-skinned sailor had made it safely ashore.

The cottage was situated just outside a tiny fishing village several miles from St Ives, on a part of the coastline so rugged and swept by dangerous tides that it had never fallen foul of any developers.

Tregellan Cottage was perched on top of a jagged stretch of cliff exposed to the full force of the Atlantic gales in the winter.

It had its own private beach that could only be reached via a narrow cliff path that was not for vertigo sufferers or those who were queasy-stomached.

There were no signs of life in the village, but Jenna had not expected there to be; at gone two in the morning it was hardly likely that anyone would still be awake.

Craig's Porsche purred triumphantly up the narrow cliff road—as her poor little Mini would never have done. The cottage was in darkness, and she parked at the front, climbing a little wearily out of the driving seat and walking towards the door.

It was a beautifully clear night and she stopped briefly to breathe in the salt-laden air.

Even from where she stood she could see the ocean—see and hear it, the soft, lulling sound of the outgoing tide distinctly soothing to the ear.

She moved, her bare arms caught by the sudden breeze that sprang up and she shivered slightly as she hurried down the flagged path to the cottage door.

She had changed into a comfortable cotton jumpsuit for the drive, and the sea wind flattened the fabric across the fullness of her breasts.

The cottage had no bell, just an old-fashioned lion-headed knocker. However, just as she lifted her hand to touch it, the cottage door opened.

It was a rather odd sensation, staring into complete blackness, and Jenna hesitated uncertainly on the threshold until common sense came to her rescue and she realised that Susie must have heard her drive up.

Stepping inside she said quickly, 'Susie, I'm afraid I've let you down and you're in for a shock...'

'Unfortunately, Jenna, I suspect the shock is going to be yours.' She gasped as Simon stepped out from the shadows. 'Please excuse the rather theatrical darkness, but I can't find the blasted paraffin lights, and the generator is on the blink.'

Electricity had never reached the remoteness of the clifftop, and for years the Townsends had kept on hand some old-fashioned storm lanterns for those occasions when the temperamental generator refused to work.

'I think your mother keeps them on the cold slab in the small cellar,' Jenna responded automatically, shock giving way to ire, as she demanded, 'What are *you* doing here, Simon? You told me you weren't going to come down until tomorrow.'

'So I did, but I changed my mind...I must admit it never struck me that you would be so quixotically loyal to my idiotic sister as to drive down here yourself! It can't have been a comfortable journey in that tin can of yours.'

'I'm not driving the Mini,' Jenna snapped. 'Craig lent me his Porsche.'

Now that her eyes were accustomed to the gloom, she could see the derisive lift of Simon's eyebrows quite clearly.

'Really? He must be more besotted than I'd imagined, or you, my lovely Jenna, must be far more... talented.'

She flushed beneath the barb of the deliberate sexual innuendo, hating him for the mockery it held.

'Unfortunately, both of us appear to have made a wasted journey, because Susie isn't here.'

'Not here! But she told me...'

'She lied to you, I'm afraid,' Simon interrupted her coolly. 'She isn't here, nor has she been here... I must admit I was a little surprised to learn that her luxury-loving friend was prepared to spend close on two weeks down here. The Côte d'Azur is more in his line.'

He said it with a hard disdain that made Jenna wince.

The burst of adrenalin which had fuelled her determined drive to Cornwall had gone. In its place was a weary exhaustion that locked her muscles and made her ache for sleep.

There was only one thing left for her to do now and that was to return to her flat. The thought of the long, tiring drive was not a tempting one.

As she turned round and started to walk away, Simon caught hold of her arm.

'Where are you going?'

'Back to London.'

She saw him grimace, a weary, almost self-mocking tightening of his facial features, which surely must only have been the trick of the light, because Simon had never viewed himself with self-mockery in all his life—of that she was quite sure.

'Rather dramatic, don't you think? I know you loathe the very sight of me, Jenna, but you're hardly going to be contaminated by spending half a dozen hours under the same roof. I shouldn't think your boyfriend would be too pleased if you wrote off that expensive piece of equipment he's loaned you. You're in no fit state to drive back to London now,' he added firmly. 'I suspect we'll find that half the bedding's damp and the cottage is freezing but, thanks to my dear sister's notorious selfishness, we have no other option but to stay here.'

Jenna frowned. *Susie* selfish!

'She didn't know we'd follow her down here. I suppose she changed her mind at the last minute and...'

'Didn't she?' Simon asked her sardonically. 'I think you'll discover that Susie never had the slightest intention of coming down here. If I'd given it more thought at the appropriate time, I should have guessed she'd given you a red herring. Susie was never overly fond of the place. She'd certainly never choose it as a lovers' rendezvous.'

'Susie loved it down here,' Jenna protested. 'We both did.'

The look Simon gave her as he turned to study her upturned face in the darkness of the hall made her feel odd—weak and vulnerable, somehow, as though she had said something very betraying.

'Susie's a city dweller,' Simon told her. 'Not like you. What made you go and live in London? I thought you were going to spend the rest of your life in Gloucestershire.'

'What as?' Jenna asked him bitterly. 'The village spinster?'

Simon ignored her gibe and added tauntingly, 'What happened to the husband and two-point-two offspring you were so convinced you wanted?'

'That was when I was fifteen—I've changed since then.'

'Yes, yes, I believe you have. Stay here, I'll go down to the cellar and get the lamps.'

Much as she objected to his high-handed manner, Jenna knew there was little point in following him down the steep flight of stone steps into the cellar.

The house was built into the cliff side, and as teenagers she and Susie had amused themselves by searching the stone rooms for secret doorways that might conceal passages down inside the cliff face, as in the best tradition of smuggling stories. Or rather, *she* had amused herself, Jenna realised painfully. Susie had always been rather inclined to scoff at her romantic imaginings.

She made her way to the larger of the cottage's two sitting-rooms, and pushed open the door. In the dim light she could see that the furniture was swathed in covers. The air smelled cold and faintly stale, and she went over to open one of the windows.

Simon was right, there was little point in her driving back to London tonight, and yet she still felt a small prickle of unease at the thought of being alone here with him. It was ironic really, when for so many years she had been filled with foolishly romantic dreams of just such an event.

How old had she been when she had become infatuated with him? Fifteen? Fifteen! Why deceive herself? she asked herself ironically. She could remember exactly when it had happened. It had been here at this very house, the summer she was fifteen. Simon had made an unexpected visit and she had been sitting in the garden when he arrived. Tall and bronzed from his French Riviera holiday, where he had been crewing on a friend's yacht, she had watched him come towards her. Jenna had been alone at the time, Susie and her parents having gone into the nearest town to do some shopping.

Her heart had almost seemed to stop beating, lurching into her throat. She hadn't been able to speak or even breathe...

Thank heavens she had managed to keep her feelings to herself, and that no one had ever guessed how

she felt. Once or twice she had felt a thrill of fear at
the thought that Simon might have realised, but apart
from the odd teasing comment, delivered in much
the same brotherly manner he used towards Susie, he
had rarely even spoken to her.

The arrival of his latest, equally tall and tanned
girlfriend had brought home to her the impossibility
of her romantic yearnings, and when towards the end
of the holiday she and Susie had become engaged in
a heated conversation about how they wanted to
spend the rest of their lives, Elena had laughed in
derision when Jenna had mentioned her own wish to
settle down and have a family.

'You see, Simon,' she had said laughingly, 'you
should always avoid quiet, plain little girls, they *always* have marriage on their minds.'

Jenna had been hurt by the older girl's cruel remark, but after all there had been nothing personal
in it. Since her arrival they had hardly seen anything
of her or Simon. They went out together every day
in Simon's small sports car, returning only briefly at
supper time to eat and change to go out again.

Her infatuation for Simon had died quite quickly,
but it had left her with a curious antipathy towards
him, an unease when in his company that made her
restless and on edge.

She heard him coming back, and heard him swear
as he stumbled into something.

'I've found the lamps, but there doesn't seem to
be any fuel for them.'

'It's in the garage,' Jenna told him.

He cursed again.

'Only a woman could do something as idiotic as that! Why on earth isn't it with the lamps?'

'Because I believe your father considered that it was safer to fill and light the lamps outside than in the confined space of the cellar,' Jenna told him coldly.

'Ah, I see… Very well then, I consider myself well and truly put in my place, and take back everything I have said about your sex, Jenna. Will that do? Have I made amends?'

'I'll go upstairs and see if I can sort out some bedding,' Jenna told him, ignoring his taunting remark. 'I wonder if your mother still keeps those sleeping-bags down here?'

'I don't know. It must be a couple of years since anyone was last down. My father was talking about selling the place.'

Jenna only just managed to suppress her instinctive protest, reminding herself that whatever Susie's family might choose to do with their cottage was really no concern of hers. But so many of the happier memories of her childhood centred round this weathered, unprotected dwelling. She was being sentimental, she told herself as she went upstairs and made her way to the small walk-in airing cupboard.

Without any proper light it was impossible to find what she was looking for, so she resigned herself to await Simon's return.

He wasn't long. She heard the door bang as he came inside, and then saw the glow from the two lamps he was carrying.

He brought one up to her, leaving the other at the foot of the stairs.

'Here, this what you're after?' he asked, tugging on the neatly folded, familiar sleeping-bags.

'Yes, I thought it would make more sense to use these than to bother making up the beds.'

'I agree. I was having a root in the kitchen before you arrived. I think I've managed to locate a jar of instant coffee and some powdered milk. Mrs M must leave it here for when she comes to do her monthly check.'

Mrs Magellan was the wife of the local garage proprietor. She had a key for the cottage and came up once a month to clean and check that all was in order.

'I thought I'd use Susie's and my room,' Jenna suggested, handing Simon one of the sleeping-bags, and turning away from him.

She and Susie had shared the smallest bedroom, tucked up under the eaves, and she headed for it instinctively.

She only realised that Simon had followed her when she saw the golden glow of the lamp reflecting against the polished wood of the door.

She turned the handle and the lamp illuminated the interior of the small room. The two single beds that once occupied it had been dismantled and an ominous dark stain covered part of the ceiling.

'Damn! I forgot... Dad did say something about the roof losing some slates during a bad storm. Let's hope that the damage is just restricted to this room.'

It wasn't... Out of the cottage's four bedrooms, only one remained damp free.

It would, of course, have to be Simon's, although his single bed had gone and in its place was the double bed that had once been in his parents' room.

'Well, Jenna,' Simon announced when they had both surveyed the room in silence, 'it looks that at long last all your girlish dreams are going to come true and you get to spend the night with me... I take it that you will...er...behave like a lady?'

Jenna could have hit him. All those years when she thought she had successfully hidden that embarrassing teenage crush from him, and now he casually let her know that she hadn't! What was more, he actually dared to taunt her with the fact, and to add insult to injury.

'Don't worry, Simon,' she told him with acid sweetness. 'I'm rather fussy about whom I sleep with—one has to be these days. You'll be quite safe... I'll sleep downstairs.'

'Oh, well, at least you won't be alone,' he responded comfortingly. 'From the signs I saw in the kitchen, it looks like a whole colony of mice have taken up residence. I suppose they must have come in from the fields.'

All her life Jenna had had an irrational fear of the small, furry creatures and now immediately she tensed, visions of an entire army of them frolicking over her recumbent form as she slept tormenting her. She shuddered.

'You're lying to me.'

Simon's eyebrows rose.

'Why on earth should I? You don't actually think I have evil designs upon you, do you?'

Put like that it sounded ridiculous. Of course he didn't want her, she knew that, but she also knew that for some reason he seemed to delight in tormenting her. Tormenting her? How could lying on the same mattress while securely wrapped up in her own sleeping-bag possibly torment her?

'Look, I'm shattered. You make whatever arrangements you choose, Jenna, but if you'll excuse me I want to get some sleep.'

'Do you want to take the lamp or...'

Reluctantly she picked up her sleeping-bag and walked over to the bed.

Behind her she heard the bedroom door swing shut and for some ridiculous reason she felt as though she had walked into a well-sprung trap.

'I'll let you have first go at the bathroom,' Simon offered magnanimously, 'but I warn you, the water is like ice.'

It came from an underground well and Jenna shivered in remembered dread of its icy sting.

She went down to the car to fetch her overnight

case, acknowledging the impossibility of using the two shaped seats as a makeshift bed. She was aching all over with tension and tiredness.

She heard Simon moving about in the kitchen as she walked in.

'Fancy a cup of cocoa? I've found some at the back of the cupboard, although heaven only knows what it will taste like with dried milk.'

She was thirsty, and perhaps it would be as well if, for this one night at least, she put her resentment of him behind her.

'Yes, please.'

'OK. I'll bring it up when it's ready.'

By the time she heard his footsteps on the stairs, she was undressed and tucked up inside her sleeping-bag. It occurred to her that in anyone other than Simon she could have taken his delay as a gentle-manly acknowledgement of her modesty, but since when had Simon ever bothered to take her feelings into account over anything?

The cocoa was surprisingly good, warming her chilled hands as she cradled the mug.

Simon disappeared into the bathroom, and was gone long enough for her to finish her drink and snuggle down into her sleeping bag.

She felt the bed dip and heard the rustle of the nylon fabric as he made himself comfortable, and then the room was plunged into darkness as he ex-tinguished the light.

Some time during the night she dreamed that she

was freezing cold, ploughing through numbing wastes of snow, and then deliciously she was warm again. She smiled in her sleep, completely unaware of the fact that the reason she was now so warm was that Simon had unzipped their separate sleeping-bags and then zipped them together to provide extra warmth.

It also brought Jenna into much closer contact with his warm body as he lay against her back!

CHAPTER THREE

JENNA heard the noise distantly, as no more than an irritating intrusion into the pleasant rosiness of her dream. She wriggled comfortably and burrowed deeper into the sleeping-bag, relishing the solid wall of warmth at her back, and then when the noise grew more intrusive she opened her eyes, blinking reluctantly in the brilliance of the early morning sunshine.

It took her several seconds to grasp what was going on. She remembered getting into bed all right, and she remembered the sleeping-bag as well, but she also distinctly recalled cocooning herself into it *alone*, and now for some reason it seemed to have stretched to include...

She tensed and turned over.

Simon!

He was still asleep, looking absurdly young, even with a dark overnight growth of beard.

'I don't know who it is in there, but you're on private property...'

The bedroom door opened unceremoniously, and Mrs Magellan stood there, glaring belligerently at the bed.

The way her expression changed as she recognised

both its occupants could in other circumstances have been amusing, but right at this moment Jenna felt more like a naughty schoolgirl caught in an underhand activity.

'Well, I never! *Miss* Jenna... And Master *Simon*...' A disapproving frown pleated Mrs Magellan's forehead. 'Well, when I saw those two cars parked outside, I thought you must be some of those hippies...I never thought...'

Her frown deepened, and Jenna wondered despairingly how on earth she was going to be able to explain the long and complicated story that was the truth.

She kicked Simon ruthlessly and hard on the shin. *He* was the one who had got them into this mess, she fumed, and he could jolly well get them out of it! He was the one with the trained legal brain, after all—the brilliant barrister so fluently capable of putting forward a good defence.

She kicked him again. He muttered something unintelligible and then opened his eyes.

'My God, Mrs M!' He sat bolt upright, exposing a good deal of hair-darkened masculine torso.

'Mrs Magellan wants to know what we're doing here, Simon,' Jenna told him.

'Ah...'

Jenna could have sworn that he was amused, though no sign of undesirable levity showed in his face.

'Well...'

'I'm sure it's not for me to question a fully grown man about his morals, Mr Simon, but I should think your mother would have something to say to this...and with Miss Jenna as well...'

'Yes, well, you see, Mrs M, Jenna and I—we're going to get married...and Jenna being the sentimental sort wanted to come down here to the place where she first fell in love with me. You know what girls are...'

At his side, Jenna seethed in bitter silence. How dared he do this to her! Why couldn't he simply have told Mrs Magellan the truth?

'Of course, we had intended to have separate rooms, but we didn't realise there'd been so much rain damage...'

'Oh, well, since the pair of you are getting married, I suppose it's all right...but it's not what I would have expected of you, Miss Jenna... I'll go downstairs now and let you both get up. I dare say you'll be wanting to get back to London once you've had a bite of breakfast.'

The moment the older woman had closed the door behind her, Jenna rounded on Simon.

'What on earth made you tell her we were getting married?' she demanded furiously. 'Why didn't you tell her the truth?'

'I didn't think she'd believe it. I thought I did quite well on the spur of the moment,' he added thoughtfully. 'Very well, in fact...'

Jenna wasn't to be mollified.

'You know what a gossip she is! It will be all round the village by tonight...'

'So what? Come on, Jenna,' he drawled, looking into her shuttered, angry face. 'It *could* be worse. I could have let her go on thinking that the pair of us had sneaked down here for a spot of illicit sex, instead of which I did the gentlemanly thing and...'

'Lied to her! Gave her a totally false impression of our relationship!' Jenna fumed.

'What's wrong? It will never get any further than the village. Your boyfriend isn't likely to find out, if that's what's bothering you.'

'It isn't,' Jenna announced shortly. 'I just don't like being involved in any sort of deceitfulness,' she told him virtuously.

His eyebrows lifted.

'And of course, lying to me about Susie's whereabouts in no way constituted any form of deceit?' he suggested softly.

Jenna wanted to hit him. In fact she was reaching out to do so, when he moved away from her and she became aware that all he was wearing appeared to be a minute pair of briefs.

'And that's another thing,' she told him bitterly. 'When I went to bed last night, I was lying alone, in my own sleeping-bag.'

'Mm... You woke me up during the night complaining that you were cold, clinging on to me for dear life. The only way I could shut you up was to zip both bags together.'

Jenna was about to make a heated retort when she had a sudden and extremely disturbing memory of dreaming about snow. She bit down hard on her bottom lip, cursing the tricks that the subconscious mind could play.

'Look, there's nothing to get so worked up about. To listen to you anyone would think this is the first time you've been to bed with a man.'

He said it so casually that Jenna was stricken into silence. Although he didn't know it, it was, but there was something so shaming about still being a virgin at twenty-four years of age that she kept it a deep and dark secret.

And the problem was that the longer her virginal state continued, the harder it was going to be to get rid of it.

'Do you want first go at the bathroom, or shall I go down first and appease Mrs M?'

'With what?' Jenna snapped. 'More lies?'

Even so, she made no objection when he got out of bed, other than to quickly turn her head, averting her eyes from his nearly nude body.

The last time she had seen him wearing so little had been the summer of her adolescent crush, but he had filled out since then, the youth's body becoming that of a man. Her stomach lurched protestingly as her senses logged the flat hardness of his belly and the tensile, muscular strength of his thighs. He leaned over her, picking up his clothes and she tensed, wishing that he wouldn't come so close to her. Such man-

to-woman intimacy was quite obviously so familiar
to him as breathing, while she…while she was ren-
dered as gauche and nervous as a schoolgirl, she
mocked herself acidly.

As he moved away from her, she heard him saying
laconically, 'It's all right, Jenna. I don't think looking at another man constitutes an act of unfaithful-
ness.'

Thank God Simon thought she was involved in a
sexual relationship with Craig. Otherwise… Otherwise what? Otherwise nothing, she told herself
firmly, waiting until she heard him going downstairs
before snatching up her own clothes and heading for
the bathroom.

It was over an hour before they could escape Mrs
Magellan's determination to provide them with a fit-
ting breakfast, and her questions about the latest
news on their families, but at last they were free to
go.

Jenna hated the way Simon insisted on accompanying her out to Craig's car. Quite what Mrs M made
of a pair of lovers who arrived at their destination in
separate vehicles she had no idea, but no doubt were
she to ask, Simon would have a response suitably
lacking in truth and reality for her.

'You're supposed to be madly in love with me
darling—remember?' he taunted her as she tried to
pull away from his constraining hand.

'Perhaps my lack of conviction springs from the

fact that it's a role I find it quite impossible to visualise myself in,' Jenna told him tartly.

'Really! You do surprise me. Can this be the same Jenna who used to follow my every movement with yearning, lovelorn glances?'

Jenna stopped abruptly.

'Why you…' She swung around, furious that he should be callous enough to refer to her youthful crush. Her heel caught in a tussock of grass as she moved, and she felt it give way beneath her.

As she fought to regain her balance she saw Simon reaching out towards her. For some reason, she thought that he was going to kiss her, and she was instantly filled with a sense of blind panic, pushing him away.

'Don't be such an idiot!' His arms restrained her. 'Or do you want to end up in the ditch?'

To her fury and embarrassment, as Jenna looked behind her she saw how close she had come to overbalancing into the overgrown ditch that ran alongside the road. She bit her lip as a flood of mortified colour stung her skin.

'Poor Jenna, it isn't your weekend, is it? Never mind. I'm sure you'll find that lover-boy is waiting to welcome you home with open arms. Known him long, have you?'

'I don't see that it's any business of yours,' Jenna snapped back at him. 'I don't question you about your love life, do I?'

One dark eyebrow rose lazily.

'Do you want to? What would you like to know?'

Oh, he really was the most exasperating man, Jenna fumed as she climbed into the Porsche and tried to analyse exactly what it was about him that drove her into such a fury of temper. She was normally such a calm, controlled person, but Simon simply had to look at her to make every slur on the temperamental nature of redheads immediately come true.

It was just as well she had been so angry, she decided half an hour later as she tried to concentrate on her driving. Otherwise there was no saying what she might have betrayed when he had revealed the fact that he had known all along about that embarrassing crush she had had on him...

Of course, it was typical of him to have said nothing all these years and then to casually drop it into the conversation like that.

She remembered one afternoon when she had inadvertently come across him and Elena lying in a secluded patch of sunwarmed grass on the cliffs.

They had been wrapped in each other's arms, Simon's long legs pressing Elena into the grass, their mouths locked into an intensely passionate kiss.

Later that night in bed, she had tried to imagine what it would be like to be kissed by Simon like that. She had never found out... And she certainly never wanted to, she told herself acidly.

He *had* tried to kiss her once: on her eighteenth birthday, at the party her grandmother had given for her, but she had been very much on her dignity, painfully aware of the huge gulf that yawned between them, her newly emerging woman's pride stung by the knowledge that, to him, kissing her was rather like kissing another sister.

She had averted her face at the last moment and his kiss had landed on her cheek.

Even then, he had had to have the last word, she remembered now, whispering tauntingly in her ear, 'No? You don't know what you're missing!'

At least having that ridiculous teenage crush on him had inured her for life against men like him. If she ever did fall in love, it would be with a far different kind of man: someone who treated her with respect and consideration, someone who did not have a long line of girlfriends marching through his past.

Her ire at Simon's high-handed and totally unnecessary behaviour lasted almost the entire length of her drive back to London.

It was late afternoon before she parked Craig's Porsche and let herself into her own flat.

As soon as she had freshened up she went up to take him his keys and found him busy in his darkroom, developing the work he had brought back with him.

'Pity you don't fancy modelling,' he told her, not for the first time. 'With your bone structure and colouring... Everything go all right?'

She made a non-committal response and thanked him for the use of his car.

'Tell you what, you can thank me properly over dinner tonight.'

Jenna stared at him. It was unlike Craig to ask her out formally. Ever since she had known him, he had used a succession of elegant models as a cloak for his love for Emma Parker. Despite his tan he was looking very gaunt, she noticed suddenly.

'Craig, is something wrong?'

'You could say that. Emma's been told that Paul only has a few months to live. I don't understand her, Jenna. All along she's insisted that she loves me, that it's only loyalty that keeps her with Paul, but now from the way she's acting, you'd think she was fathoms deep in love with the guy. She won't speak to me, she won't answer my letters or phone calls. When I went round to see her, she told her house-keeper not to let me in. Why? I just don't understand it.'

'She's bound to be confused at the moment, Craig. Why don't you just give her a breathing space?'

She didn't want to say to him that Emma might possibly be suffering from a feeling of guilt, and that the imminence of her husband's death could have temporarily overwhelmed her love for Craig.

She left him looking morose and very unhappy, having accepted his invitation to dinner.

She didn't particularly want to go. For one thing she was still suffering from the traumatic effects of her journey to Cornwall, and for another she had been half hoping that Susie might ring.

Where on earth had her friend gone? Had Susie actually known that Simon would come round to her flat? She knew she ought to be annoyed with her, but somehow she lacked the energy.

THE RESTAURANT Craig took her to had only recently opened. Its financial backer was a well-known script-writer, and so it attracted a good many well-known faces from TV and stage shows.

Privately Jenna considered both the décor and the manner of many of the other diners to be slightly overdone, although she could not fault the service nor the appetising selection of dishes on the menu.

'The chef trained with the Roux brothers,' Craig told her, 'and I've been told that the food is excellent.'

Excellent it indeed was, but that did not stop Craig from merely toying with what he had ordered.

He *had* lost weight, Jenna noticed, studying him with faint alarm, suddenly very concerned for him.

What would happen if Emma's guilt over Paul's death led to her rejecting Craig permanently? He had loved her for so long... Since before she and Paul had married, he had once told her. All three of them had been at university together. He and Emma had been on the point of becoming engaged when they had had a quarrel, over his desire to travel and work abroad.

He had left for France without her, and when he came back she had married Paul.

Jenna watched as he pushed his food around his plate, wishing there was some way she could help him, but knowing that there was not.

Love could be such a hurting, bitter thing… She frowned, trying to shake off the mood of depression threatening to swamp her.

She had never been in love. She had been spared its agonies and ecstasies, apart from that brief teenage crush on Simon, and that had not really been love.

She frowned again, annoyed with herself for allowing him to take up so much space in her thoughts. Seeing him again so unexpectedly had unsettled her. The wide chasm that had yawned between them when she was fifteen and he was in his early twenties seemed disconcertingly to have disappeared, and she recognised that she had been all too conscious of him as a very male man. It was an awareness she didn't want, and consequently she found that she had as little appetite for her meal as Craig had for his.

She wasn't sorry when he pushed his plate away abruptly and said, 'This isn't a success… Let's go home, shall we?'

Most of the early diners had left and the restaurant was just beginning to fill up again with the post-theatre crowd.

As they reached the exit, Craig stood back to allow two people to pass them.

Jenna stiffened as she recognised Simon.

'Leaving already?' he questioned, eyeing her mockingly.

Perhaps it was something to do with the taunting smile he gave her, or perhaps it was the condescending, dismissing look in the eyes of his elegant female companion, Jenna didn't know, but she heard herself saying softly, 'Yes, we both wanted an early night, didn't we, darling?' She reached for Craig's hand, while gazing up into his eyes with a look of simpering adoration.

A raised eyebrow, another cool smile and they were gone, leaving her feeling as limp as a week-old lettuce.

'Well, now, what was all that about?' Craig asked as they walked out into the summer night.

'It would take far too long to explain,' Jenna told him.

'Do you realise that that's the first time that you've ever displayed any signs that you're as human as the rest of us, Jenna? I'd begun to get a little worried about you. Who is he?'

'The brother of a friend of mine.'

'Umm...I wonder where he's going to pop up again. These things always go in threes... First the flat, now the restaurant...'

For some reason, the look he was giving her made Jenna blush a vivid pink.

'He doesn't mean anything to me, Craig,' she said crossly. 'He's just the brother of an old friend...'

'Hence the small by-play in the restaurant? Come on, Jen. I know you better than that...'

'All right, so I once had a king-size crush on him, but that was years ago...'

Why on earth was she telling Craig all this? Angrily she dismissed Simon from her thoughts.

'I recognised the woman with him, of course,' Craig continued.

He mentioned the name of the woman Susie said that her brother was involved with, and Jenna shrugged her shoulders and said dismissively, 'I really don't know anything about his private life, Craig. As I said, he's just the brother of an old friend.'

They parted outside the door to Jenna's flat. The events of the previous evening had caught up with her and she was achingly tired.

By twelve o'clock she was in bed and deeply asleep.

THE TELEPHONE woke her, its shrill, insistent ring penetrating through the mists of sleep. She reached for the receiver and mumbled into it.

'Jenna, my dear! At last... I can't tell you how excited and delighted we all are.'

The bubbling voice of Susie's mother on the other end of the telephone line made Jenna sit up.

'Of course, it was very wicked of you and Simon to keep it to yourselves. Mrs M was quite put out when she rang me up about it. I rather think she disapproved of the two of you spending the weekend alone together at the cottage. I hope you don't mind, but I've already spoken to your grandmother. I just couldn't wait... It's what I've always longed for, to have you as a second daughter... I can admit now how much I was dreading Simon bringing home entirely the wrong sort of person. Of course, the gossip columns do tend to exaggerate these things, but I really had no idea that you and he... But that doesn't matter now. I just want you to know how thrilled we are about it. I told Simon as much when I rang him earlier. When will the wedding be? Of course, you'll be having it here at home... Oh, heavens! I am running on, aren't I? But I just can't tell you how pleased we are, Jenna...'

Appalled, Jenna stared blankly at the receiver. What on earth was going on? Slowly her numb brain accepted the fact that Simon's mother appeared to think that she and Simon were engaged.

Why on earth hadn't Simon told her the truth? How *could* he let his mother go on thinking that there was something between them?

She opened her own mouth to tell her and then closed it firmly again. Why should she do his dirty work? He could do it himself. After all, *he* was the one who had got them into this mess in the first place...telling Mrs M all those lies. He might have known that the first thing she would do would be to ring his parents.

These and other thoughts rioted through her brain in a confused mingling of shock and anger.

She must have said something to Ellen Townsend, but, for the life of her, when she eventually replaced the receiver she had no idea what it was.

She wasn't exactly at her best first thing on a Monday morning in any case. Her alarm hadn't even gone off yet...her alarm! Too late, she remembered that she had forgotten to set it the night before. A glance at her watch confirmed her fear that she was about to be late for work.

She got up and raced round, showering, dressing, putting on her make-up, wondering what on earth had happened to her normal, well organised and calm, ordered life.

It was Simon's fault. Until he had appeared in it, her life had run on smooth, well-functioning lines, and now suddenly it was racketing out of control and heading for what promised to be a spectacular crash.

She was late for work, arriving flustered and breathless to find her boss pacing her office, his forehead carved into a heavy frown.

Luckily it didn't take her long to appease him, but they had a heavy workload on, and she had to forgo her lunch hour to get her desk clear.

By mid-afternoon she had managed to persuade herself that she must have imagined this morning's telephone call from Susie's mother, but as the day wore on, her persuasion became less convincing.

What on earth was she going to do? And it wasn't

just Susie's parents who would have to be told the truth, there was her grandmother as well. Her heart gave an unpleasant lurch as she digested this thought.

Her grandmother had always had a soft spot for Simon—more than merely a soft spot if the truth were known—and now she would be thinking that she was shortly to get him as her grandson-in-law. Jenna stared at the telephone on her desk, itching to pick it up and put a call through to her, but her grandmother didn't hear very well these days, and besides, wasn't it something that it would be easier to explain in person?

Coward, she scorned herself. You know you just don't want to tell her, to disappoint her...

But she would have to be told some time. This weekend, Jenna promised herself, she would go down and see her this weekend, and explain everything... Her mind made up, she felt a little less guilty, although she was still furious with Simon.

By the time she got home she was hot and tired, longing only for a cool shower and an early night. Craig had gone up to the Lakes for several days on a shoot, and so she had the house to herself.

She had her shower first, briskly towelling herself dry, and leaving her hair loose and damp.

A huge rugby shirt she had filched from Craig was her favourite relaxing at home wear, but it was too hot for the jeans she normally wore with it.

The flat was stuffy after being closed up all day, and she had opened all the windows and propped

open the back door to get as much through draught
as possible. Summer in the city was impossible, especially when the weather was like this—hot and
sticky. She thought yearningly of home, and even
more yearningly of Cornwall. She was due to take a
month's holiday shortly, but she had no idea what
she was going to do with it. She had half hoped to
persuade Susie to go away with her, but she had had
tentative thoughts of spending a week at home with
Gran... She shrugged as she went into the kitchen to
prepare her supper.

She would eat it outside tonight. She was having
tuna fish salad. She had just finished pouring out a
mug of coffee and was about to pick up her tray
when a shadow fell across the open kitchen door.

'Eating alone? Where's lover-boy tonight?'

'Simon!'

She almost dropped the tray. She had been so en-
grossed in her thoughts that she hadn't heard him
walk through the small backyard.

'What are you doing here?' she demanded crossly.
'Why didn't you ring the front doorbell? And for
your information Craig is *not* my lover—we're just
friends, that's all.'

Heaven alone knew what had made her add that
last comment—possibly the cynicism carved deep
into the lines round his mouth when he drawled it,
she didn't know.

His eyebrows rose slightly.

'That's just as well, since you and I are now virtually engaged.'

Something in his voice made her stiffen and look at him.

'That's hardly *my* fault,' she reminded him bitterly. 'You were the one who spun Mrs M that ridiculous fairytale. You should have known that she'd ring your mother!'

'Ah, so she has spoken to you?'

'To *me*, to my *grandmother*, to *half* the village by now, I expect,' Jenna said bitterly. 'It obviously hasn't occurred to you, Simon, that I might not relish the idea of being married off to you, without...'

He interrupted her calmly, 'Since it's unlikely to happen, may I suggest that you're rather overreacting.'

Jenna exploded.

'*I'm* overreacting? *You* spoke to your mother! Why didn't you tell her that it was a mistake?'

'Why didn't *you*?'

Jenna stared at him, perplexed.

'Look, I'll be honest with you. At the moment it would suit me very nicely to have a fictitious fiancée, and that's one of the reasons why I didn't tell Ma the truth straight away.' He looked directly at her, a rather odd gleam in his eyes, as he added softly, 'The other one was that she was so damned thrilled with the idea that I simply didn't have the heart.'

There was something about the way he was looking at her that was having a distinctly odd effect on her heartbeat. Try as she might, she couldn't seem to disentangle herself from the dangerously exciting sensation racing through her veins. She couldn't even manage to look away from him, she realised on a breathless start of surprise.

'That's a very fetching outfit you're wearing, by the way,' Simon commented softly. 'Just the sort of thing to make a fiancé very eager to become a bridegroom.'

It was impossible to stop the wild sweep of colour running up over her skin as she looked down and realised what he meant.

The oversized shirt stopped midway down her thighs, revealing the long, slim length of her legs. All she was wearing underneath it was a brief pair of panties, and somehow, although that fact wasn't immediately obvious, she suspected that Simon knew. She lifted a hand defensively to the tumbled heaviness of her hair, and then checked herself, sanity returning.

She was behaving like an adolescent idiot. Simon wanted something from her and he was trying to bemuse her into a state where she would willingly go along with whatever it was he was planning. Well, it wasn't going to work!

'We're in the nineteen-eighties, Simon,' she told him grittily. 'Celibacy is out—remember? Engaged couples are as free to make love as married ones. And I don't care what would suit you—I want this whole thing sorted out and our families told the truth.'

She waited for him to try and persuade her to change her mind, tensing as she felt him move behind her. She could feel the heat coming off his body and waited in dreadful anticipation of his touch against her skin.

She felt his breath against her shoulder, even through the thickness of her shirt, one of his hands lightly cupping the ball of her shoulder joint as he leaned forward. He was going to kiss her, to try and persuade her...

'Mm...raw carrot...lovely!'

He reached past her, helping himself to some of the carrot sticks off her plate. Jenna couldn't believe it. Her body sagged with relieved outrage.

'Well, if you won't help me then you won't,' he said good-temperedly. 'I'll leave it to you to tell the folks and your grandmother, shall I? After all, you know me—I might get it all wrong!'

He was blackmailing her, that was what he was doing, and he knew it, damn him! He was standing there in her kitchen, filching her supper, looking at her with that bland, amused expression in his eyes, registering every furious, defensive movement of her body...knowing that he had her trapped.

Call it weakness, call it stupidity, call it what you liked, she knew there was no way she could destroy the pleasure she had heard in his mother's voice by telling her that she had got it all wrong and that they weren't about to get engaged. No way at all!

She could feel herself weakening.

'We'll have to tell them some time.'

'Of course! But we'll let them down lightly, shall we? I'll tell you what, how about letting them see us together at close quarters, so that they can realise for themselves how unsuited we are?'

It sounded like a good idea, but it rolled off his tongue too patly, and she was immediately suspicious.

'What do you mean? How can we do that, when we're both here in London and our families live sixty miles away?'

'Quite easily. My parents have rented a house in the Dordogne for the summer. I promised them that I'd join them for a couple of weeks or so. I know from Susie that you've got some holidays due...'

'You mean, you want us to spend a holiday in France with your parents?'

'My parents and your grandmother. I'm sure two weeks or so of observing us at close quarters will convince all three of them exactly how unsuited we are.'

'What about your latest lady?' Jenna asked suspiciously. 'What's she going to say about you spending a fortnight or more posing as someone else's fiancé, or won't you tell her?'

'Oh, I shall tell her,' Simon said silkily, and Jenna knew instantly from his expression that there was more to this whole charade than a simple desire to please his parents.

'You want her to think you're involved with someone else, don't you?'

He smiled sardonically at her.

'Full marks—go to the top of the class.'

'I've thought a lot of things about you, Simon, but I never thought you lacked the honesty to tell a woman that you no longer wanted her,' she told him acidly.

What was the matter with her? She should be delighted by this evidence of his duplicity and lack of character, but instead she felt a small stab of very real pain.

'I have told her,' he contradicted flatly. 'But with some women actions speak louder than words.'

A look crossed his face that Jenna couldn't wholly interpret, and she suffered a sensation almost as though the earth beneath her feet shifted a little. There had been such a bleak emptiness in Simon's eyes for a moment, such an aura of pain about the tightness of his mouth that she almost reached out to comfort him. That look had not been the look of a man bored with a woman he no longer wanted, but that of a man who had suffered and still suffered the anguish of loving a woman who did not love him in return.

The thought of that happening to Simon of all men was so startling that she forgot to question him further, simply turning away from him so that he wouldn't see the compassion in her eyes.

'All right, I'll go along with you...but we'll have to tell them before the holiday's over, Simon.'

'Don't worry. I'm sure by that time they'll be under no illusions as to how we feel about one another. That salad doesn't look very inviting. How about letting me take you out for a meal so that we can celebrate?'

'Celebrate what?'

'Why, our engagement, of course! What else?'

It took her several seconds to recover from the faint tingle of delight she felt inside.

Ruthlessly suppressing it, she said severely, 'Certainly not! I'm tired, and I want an early night.'

She wondered if he would make some joking remark about their supposed engaged state and perhaps kiss her, but he didn't and she wasn't prepared to admit after he had gone that the feeling she was experiencing was one of disappointment.

CHAPTER FOUR

JENNA knew that something had changed the moment she woke up, but she couldn't remember what it was. She struggled for several seconds to recall the cause of the odd feeling of anger and exhilaration that coursed through her veins, and then when she did she sat bolt upright in bed. She was engaged to Simon!

Disgusted with herself, she flopped back against the pillows, pushing her hair back with an impatiently graceful gesture. Why on earth should that make her feel exhilarated? She disliked Simon and she always had!

But she also enjoyed their little spats; he challenged her, deliberately so, she thought at times, and every time she rose to that challenge she felt the adrenalin surge through her veins.

Telling herself that it was far too early in the morning for this unwanted mood of introspection, she slid slim legs from beneath the quilt and hurried into her bathroom.

Half-way there she stopped dead. She was engaged...engaged to Simon! Impossible! But true, none the less, and what was worse, what she had momentarily lost sight of in her inner struggle to deny the complexity of her feelings towards him, was the fact that she had recklessly committed herself to spending almost the entire month of July with him.

She was cravenly wondering how she could back out of going when the phone rang. She put down the piece of toast she was nibbling and picked up the receiver.

'Jenna, my dear! I'm sorry to bother you at this time in the morning, but Simon rang me last night to tell me that both of you will be joining us in the Dordogne. He thought it might be a good idea if I rang and gave you a few details. Luckily, the cottage will be large enough for all of us...when we booked it we were anticipating both Susie and a friend of Simon's, John Cameron, would be coming.' There was a small pause and Jenna, still blurry with sleep, yawned, shock jolting through her body as Ellen Townsend said delicately and rather uncomfortably, 'I'm not an old-fashioned mother, Jenna, but I do hope you'll understand when I say that I'll be giving you and Simon separate rooms.'

Jenna nearly dropped the receiver. Of *course* she'd be giving them separate rooms! And then the penny dropped and she gulped nervously.

'Of course, I've already told Simon this, and he quite understands, but when I said that I'd leave it to him to tell you, he said that he would prefer me to discuss it with you...'

No wonder Mrs Townsend sounded both uncertain

and embarrassed, Jenna thought gritting her teeth. She'd like to ring Simon's neck…no, worse than that…she'd like him to suffer a slow and preferably horrible death! How dared he intimate to his mother that she might not be willing to accept the latter's embargo on their sleeping together! She could hear a strange sound and it was several seconds before she realised it was the noise she was making grinding her teeth.

'Jenna, are you still there my dear?'

'Yes… Yes…'

'And you—you do understand? I realise how much in love you and Simon are, and of course…but you see your grandmother will be with us and—'

Damn Simon! Damn him to hell for putting her in this horrendous position. There was nothing she wanted more than to tell Ellen Townsend just how little desire she had for her precious son, but she and Simon had made a bargain, and she was not going to be the one to go back on her word.

'Of course I do,' she agreed, forcing a smile into her voice. 'And after all, it isn't as though it will be very long before we're married. Simon wants us to have a very short engagement…'

There, let him wriggle out of that one, Jenna thought acidly as she let his mother digest her comment.

A little to her surprise, Mrs Townsend seemed to accept it very well.

'Some time in September,' she suggested enthu-

siastically. 'The church always looks so lovely at
Harvest Festival time...'

'I really must run,' Jenna interjected hastily. 'I
don't want to be late for work.'

'Oh, well then, let me give you the dates we'll be
at the cottage,' Ellen Townsend said more practically. 'Simon told me that he'd be making all the
arrangements for your travel. Your grandmother and
I are delighted that you'll be spending the entire
month with us...I just hope you aren't going to find
it too remote. It's several kilometres from the nearest
town, right in the heart of the country. I was a bit
worried that you and Simon might be bored—both
of you seem to live such hectic lives in London, but
he assured me that you'll both enjoy the rest. Engagements can be such a trying time. I remember
ours... But I mustn't keep you. I'll look forward to
seeing you in France, Jenna...'

She had another frantically busy morning at work,
not made any easier by the fact that her boss phoned
just as she was about to take her lunch hour, asking
her to call round at the flat he was working on to
bring him some colour samples he had left behind.

The flat was in Knightsbridge, and rather than
walk she got a taxi. The fabric sample books Rick
had asked for were heavy, and she didn't feel like
carting them through the busy London streets.

This particular commission had come to them
through the good offices of another client. The flat

belonged to an American businessman who required a *pied-à-terre* in London.

The flat was at the top of a small, but very prestigious block, and this would be the first time Jenna had seen it. She often accompanied Rick in the early stages of a new commission, following him round and taking notes on his initial impressions, but this time their client had stressed that he wanted the work completed very quickly, and so there had been no time for Rick to make his usual leisurely scrutiny.

A doorman let her into the plate glass and marble foyer, when she had explained who she was, and directed her over to the lift.

Just as she was about to get into it a man sprinted across the foyer, obviously in something of a rush.

He smiled at Jenna when she held the lift for him, a flash of immaculate white teeth in a well-tanned face, his dark brown eyes a startling contrast to his wheat-blond hair.

American without doubt, Jenna decided after one discreet inspection. With those perfect teeth he couldn't possibly be anything else.

She saw him glance surreptitiously at the thin gold watch strapped to his wrist, and frown slightly as the lift started to rise.

He was standing close enough to her for her to be immediately aware of the fact that he wasn't as tall as Simon, and probably a little more thickset. Possibly seven or eight years older as well, but still a very attractive man. She had always had a weakness for blonds. She grinned a little to herself at her thoughts, and pondered the identity of that exceptionally clever woman who had first put it into the male mind that it was men who did the pursuing. Not that she had ever run after any man—but possibly only because she had not yet met one who tempted her to do so, she thought wryly. Nor did she feel she was likely to, at the grand old age of twenty-four, almost twenty-five.

Even so, this good-looking American... She glanced at him briefly, wondering if he had any hang ups about twenty-four-year-old virgins, and then the lift stopped abruptly. So abruptly that she was flung forward slightly.

He caught her, restoring her to her balance with gentlemanly concern.

Her face pink with mortification, Jenna stammered her thanks. The lift doors swished open and Rick was standing there, a frown on his face.

It cleared as he saw her.

'Ah, Jenna! Marvellous! Hello, Grant. Let me introduce you to my secretary, Jenna Armstrong. Jenna, meet our new client, Grant Freeman.'

So she had been right. He *was* an American.

Jenna remained discreetly in the background as the two men discussed the décor of the flat. Since Rick hadn't dismissed her, she guessed that he must want her to stay.

'I'd like to suggest lunch,' Grant Freeman announced with another frowning glance at his watch, 'but I'm afraid I just don't have time. What about dinner tonight? We can go through your suggestions for the décor more thoroughly then...'

'I'm afraid I can't make it,' Rick apologised. 'I already have an engagement this evening.'

'And I fly back to the States first thing in the morning. I know—' He turned to look at Jenna. '—Why don't I take your assistant to dinner, and she can put me in the picture...'

Jenna felt acutely self-conscious with both them studying her. She could sense Rick's surprise, and then his shrewd, comprehending glance swept her and he said easily, 'Yes, of course... I'll brief her beforehand, and she'll have all the information you need.'

'Great. I'll pick you up at eight, Jenna...'

She gave him her address, thoroughly bemused by the unexpected turn of events, and then he was gone, promising Rick that he would ring him from New York to advise him of the timing of his next visit.

For a few moments after he had gone there was silence, and then raising his eyebrows slightly, Rick commented, 'You seem to have made a hit there, Jenna.'

'He's only taking me to dinner so that he can discuss the décor of this place.'

Rick's eyebrows lifted.

'My dear girl,' he drawled softly, 'if you believe that, you'll believe that there are fairies at the bottom of the garden. He doesn't give a damn about the décor of this place. He's already virtually given me *carte blanche*. All he came here for today was to tell me that he wanted to take possession at the beginning of October.'

Jenna didn't try to argue. After all, it was very flattering to be asked out to dinner by such an attractive man.

Grant was picking her up at eight o'clock, and she was ready at five to. Dinner, he had said, and she had dressed accordingly in a silk wrap dress in a shade of blue that made a vivid contrast to her hair.

The evening was warm enough for her not to need a coat, and the fact that Grant arrived promptly on the dot of eight added to her good opinion of him.

He was driving a very solid and expensive-looking Mercedes, which he told her he had hired for the duration of his stay. He was staying at the Connaught, he told her, and Jenna was duly impressed.

She felt a small flare of unease when he told her that they would be dining there, but just because they were dining at his hotel, that did not necessarily mean that he was anticipating taking her up to his room immediately thereafter.

Even so, Jenna subjected him to a discreet but thoughtful scrutiny as he drove towards the Connaught, wondering if she was imagining that slightly self-indulgent and wilful curve to his mouth.

Well, he was a rich man, and like all rich men he no doubt thought his money entitled him to having whatever he wanted from life whenever he wanted it.

If the need should arise, she would simply have to discreetly but firmly disabuse him of the idea that she was sexually available.

The dining-room of the Connaught was busy, but they were shown to a table immediately. The head waiter arrived with menus, and Jenna declined Grant's offer of a pre-dinner drink. She noticed that he opted for a martini, giving the wine waiter explicit instructions as to how he wanted it made.

'I think today must have been my lucky day,' he commented when they were alone. 'It isn't often I get to ride in a lift with such a beautiful woman.'

Although privately Jenna considered that his flattery was a little heavy-handed, she smiled noncommittally, wondering why she should suddenly picture Simon's mocking smile! What was wrong with her? She had accepted his invitation willingly enough. Yes, but now she was not so sure that that had been wise. There was a look in his eyes she mistrusted. Simon—forget Simon, she chastised herself quickly. She doubted that he was thinking about her. She had half expected him to ring her following his mother's telephone call, but obviously he had not deemed it necessary, and that had irritated her. Who did he think he was? Calmly taking over her life, telling her that they were engaged, committing her to a holiday she did not want, and to a relationship she most *certainly* did not want...

'What did I say?' Grant demanded, breaking into her thoughts. 'You're looking very fierce.'

It was on the tip of her tongue to say that she was thinking about her fiancé, just to see what his reaction would be, but she stopped herself, wondering why it was she had felt the need to invoke Simon's name and his imaginary status in her life. After all, she had accepted Grant's invitation to dinner quite freely, hadn't she? If she was now having second thoughts...

She was, although they sprang more from instinct than any real reason he had given her to think that he was expecting her to pay for what would be a very expensive dinner by going to bed with him.

If she had had such doubts, she ought never to have accepted his invitation, she told herself crossly, and then immediately remembered that their dinner did have another purpose, and fished in her bag for the notes she had made on Rick's plans for the décor of the flat.

Although Grant expressed an interest, it was very lukewarm. He seemed determined to turn the conversation on to more personal lines.

Jenna was barely aware of what she had ordered to eat, and perversely she blamed Simon for the situation she was in. If it hadn't been for him, she would never have relaxed her rule about dating men she didn't really know.

Already she was anticipating that the evening would end in the kind of scene she most disliked, and Rick wouldn't be too pleased with her either...perhaps it was just as well she was going on holiday for a month!

Their first course had been served and removed, and she had barely touched hers. The second arrived, and as Jenna took her first mouthful she lifted her head, alerted by some sixth sense she seemed to have developed, and found herself staring right into Simon's eyes.

He was sitting three yards away, directly facing her. His companions, another man and two women, were not familiar to Jenna.

'Is something wrong?'

Grant reached across the table, placing his hand on her arm, concern etching a frown across his forehead.

'No—that is—I feel sick—' she lied, seizing on the excuse he had unwittingly given her. And it wasn't entirely untrue. She did feel sick, and more sick by the minute, because Simon was walking towards them, quite plainly intent on speaking to her.

'Hello, darling, what a surprise!'

His hand on her shoulder pressed her into her seat, as his mouth grazed her forehead, his casual greeting completely throwing her.

Across the table Jenna could see Grant's confused anger. Simon straightened up and extended his hand to the other man.

'Simon Townsend,' he introduced himself. 'And you must be Grant Freeman. Jenna told me that she had a business dinner this evening, but I had no idea you would be dining here...'

Jenna could feel herself gaping. She had told him no such thing... How on earth...?

'Look, when you've finished eating, why don't you join us? I'm here with some colleagues. We've been discussing a particularly difficult case we're all involved in, and I must say I would welcome my fiancée's company...'

Jenna could almost feel Grant's shock.

She felt Simon take hold of her left hand and lift it towards his lips.

'I really must get you a ring, darling. Call it chauvinistic of me if you will, to want to decorate you with my badge of possession, but I'm afraid the male sex is like that. Wouldn't you agree, Grant?'

He left, having released Jenna's hand and kissed her fingertips lightly, returning to his own table.

'I didn't realise you were engaged.'

Grant was all stiff distance, and Jenna knew that she ought to be grateful to Simon for getting her out of a potentially embarrassing situation, but all she could do was to sit there and seethe. How dared he claim her as his fiancée in front of someone else! How dared he calmly announce that they were engaged, when for all he knew she might have wanted to go to bed with Grant!

In an attempt to salvage something of the evening, Jenna returned to the notes Rick had given her, and this time Grant did not try to turn the conversation into more personal channels.

Jenna suspected that both of them were relieved when the meal was finally over. She refused Grant's offer of a liqueur, and when he stood up and excused himself, explaining that he had an early flight in the morning, she stood up with him, fully intending to leave the hotel without any further contact with Simon.

She had reckoned without his sharp eyes. The moment she stood up he was at her side, his hand on her arm giving her no option but to follow him across to where his companions still sat at their table.

On the way over she hissed furiously at him, 'Quite a coincidence, you dining here tonight of all nights.'

'No coincidence, Jenna. When I rang your office and they told me you had left early because you were dining with a client, it didn't take long to work out that since said client was staying here he would give you dinner in the hotel restaurant. So much more convenient for his bedroom...'

She stiffened beneath the grip of his fingers, her eyes glittering with fury.

'How dare you suggest that Grant wanted...'

'To take you to bed? Of course he did.' Simon seemed more amused than annoyed. 'I must say I felt quite sorry for him when he realised that someone else had a prior claim. And after he'd bought you that expensive meal as well...'

'If you knew what he wanted, why did you come over? I'm not your property, Simon. You had no right to interfere...'

'You mean that rather sickly smile you had pinned to your face wasn't because you'd just realised what you'd got yourself into?' he mocked.

Jenna could have hit him, but wisely she refrained.

'All right, Mr Know-it-all! But I *don't* want to join your friends, Simon. I'm going home.'

'Not yet, you're not...'

He wouldn't let her go, propelling her relentlessly towards the table.

A waiter brought up another chair. Drinks and coffee were ordered, and Jenna either had to sit down or look an absolute idiot by walking away.

Simon's fellow diners were another barrister and his wife, and a solicitor with whom Simon had recently been working on a case.

All three of them made her feel very welcome, and to her relief Simon introduced her as an old family friend.

She might actually have been able to enjoy herself if Simon hadn't taken advantage of the diversion created by the others' animated conversation to whisper in her ear, 'There, aren't you enjoying this much more than going to bed with your American friend?'

She ached to repudiate his mocking comment, but in all honesty knew she could not. Even so, his superiority, the way he was mocking her, the way he dared to interfere in her life, were all insupportable, and she wanted to show him as much. Since she could hardly simply get up and walk away, she did the next best thing, manoeuvring her glass so that its entire contents spilt into her lap.

It soaked straight through the silk, spreading into a huge stain.

Jenna sprang up immediately, refusing the gentlemanly offers of clean handkerchiefs to mop it up, and the waiter's solicitous concern.

'No, please, it's my own fault for being so clumsy. Simon will confirm that it's always been a fault of mine. I think I'd better go straight home, before I do any more damage...'

'Luckily it's only white wine,' the other women commiserated.

'Yes,' Simon agreed in a murmur against her ear. 'What would you have done if there had only been red?'

To her shock she then heard him saying, 'Please excuse me, everyone. I'd better see this careless young lady home, and make sure she doesn't throw herself under the wheels of a taxi...'

General laughter greeted his remark, and no one made any attempt to delay him.

'I don't need you to come with me,' Jenna muttered furiously.

'My dear, I'm your fiancé. Think how bad it would look if I left you to go home on your own. Think what my mother would say—not to mention your grandmother.'

Jenna ground her teeth. 'We are *not* engaged!'

But they were standing in the foyer—and Simon was saying something to the doorman. Before she could pull away from him someone had brought round his Aston Martin.

'In you get,' he instructed her, giving her a small push.

She loathed domineering men, Jenna decided as she was forced to get into the car. Loathed and hated them... When she married, it would be to a man who respected her views, who treated her as an equal, respected her intellect... Why was it, then, that this paragon should suddenly emerge through the channels of her imagination as a bespectacled, weedy-looking character, with a hang-dog expression?

Conditioning, she told herself wrathfully, that's what it was. All her life she had...all her life... She foundered helplessly in a confusing morass of thoughts as her imagination tormented her with another mental picture, this time of Simon. Of course he was not her ideal of all that a man should be. How could he be? She hated him! Loathed him!

'Okay, out you get!'

They were parked outside the small Chelsea mews house where Simon lived. She stared at the door bemusedly.

'I thought you were taking me home...'

'I shall later, when I've got you dried out, and you and I have got one or two things straight.'

Suspicion straightened her spine. 'Such as?'

'Inside,' Simon told her. 'There isn't enough room in here for me to avoid you if you take it into your head to throw things at me, Red.'

'Red'—that did it. The sound of that mocking, youthful taunt on his lips sent her into an immediate fury. She was out of the car and accompanying him up the steps to his front door before she realised what was happening.

No one called her 'Red'! She hated it. Just as she hated all those unjust accusations about the mercurial state of her temper.

'Working up a good head of steam, are you?' Simon approved, as he opened the door. 'That's my girl. Keep it up and you'll be all dried out in no time.'

She ached to hit him. No, not hit him—to throw something, something expensive and noisy. Yes, that was what she needed. She looked around the small sitting-room of Simon's house, and her eye lighted on a very pretty pair of china ornaments. They were antique and far too expensive and delightful to break, she decided regretfully.

'Why don't you go upstairs and take off your dress? I'll find you something to wear while it dries.'

She knew the layout of the house from previous visits with Susie. Upstairs there were two bedrooms, each with its own bathroom, and she headed automatically for the one she knew to be spare.

It had obviously been redecorated since her last visit. The pretty, feminine wallpaper was gone, and in its place was a distinctly masculine décor of rich maroon and French blue.

She stripped off her damp dress, grimacing slightly at the chilly stickiness of her skin.

She had no idea what Simon wanted to talk to her about but, having practically abducted her and brought her here, he would just have to wait while she washed the smell of wine off her skin.

The guest bathroom, too, had been altered. Now it had a large deep tub, practically big enough to fit two.

Jenna stepped out of her tights and washed the sticky residue of the wine from her legs. She had no idea what Simon was going to give her to wear. Clad only in her thin silk bra and panties, she walked into the bedroom, intending to call down to him.

As she did so, the door opened, and he walked in, coming to an abrupt halt when he saw her.

Her attempts to conceal her nearly nude body from him were pathetically juvenile, she told herself afterwards, and it was obvious that he thought so too, because once he recovered from his shock a rather odd smile lightened the darkness of his eyes.

'It's normally considered good manners to knock before walking into someone's bedroom,' Jenna told him pettishly.

'Not when the bedroom is one's own,' Simon countered.

Jenna wasn't going to stand for that. 'You knew I

was up in your guest-room. You told me to come up here... You knew...'

'This isn't the guest-room,' Simon told her, calmly interrupting her tirade.

'Of course it is. I remember when Susie and I...'

Jenna looked round uncertainly, remembering how much the décor of the room had changed.

'It used to be the guest-room,' Simon agreed patiently, 'but I found the noise from the traffic disturbed my sleep, so I changed them round.'

'You might have told me!'

'And miss the sight of you standing there in all your glory?'

He was teasing her, and it infuriated her. She could feel the hot colour stinging her skin as her rage flooded through her.

'You know, you haven't changed much at all,' Simon mused leaning against the closed door and watching her in amusement. 'I remember the first time we all went on holiday together. You must have been about twelve. We were all getting changed on the beach...'

Jenna remembered it, too. She had been so embarrassed, because she had been the only one not to have her swimsuit on under her jeans and top. Mrs Townsend had briskly produced a towelling tent for her to slip on and change under, but she had still felt awkward and embarrassed. Susie had laughed at her embarrassment, greatly amused to realise that it was caused by Simon.

'I thought you were going to give me something to wear,' she reminded him, checking her thoughts.

'Yes, so I was.' He walked past her and opened a cupboard, removing one of his shirts.

'Here, this should do the trick. Where's your dress? I'll hang it in the airing cupboard. That should dry it quickly.'

'It's over there, but I haven't sponged it yet.'

She wished he would go away. The shirt he had given her had been laundered and was buttoned all down the front. He might have done the gentlemanly thing and unbuttoned it for her, instead of lolling against the door, watching her as though for all the world they were, in reality, lovers.

She wanted to demand that he went away, and yet somehow the words wouldn't come. She was frightened of looking even more of an idiot than she already did, she realised bitterly. Simon always made her feel acutely aware of her own lack of sexual experience in comparison to his abundance of it, and she was terrified of somehow betraying that lack of it to him.

Why on earth it should matter if she did, she had no idea, but it did.

She had turned her back to him while she unfastened the shirt, all too uncomfortably aware of the fact that her silk panties and bra did almost nothing to conceal her body.

As she slid the shirt on, her fingers shook. She turned round and for a moment was transfixed. That couldn't be Simon staring at her like a man thirsting after water in the dryness of the desert; like a man tormented by a hunger he knew he could never appease.

She blinked and the moment was gone—like a mirage—and a mirage was most definitely what it had been, she told herself scathingly.

What was she thinking about? That would be the day, when Simon looked at her with desire. To him she was still a lanky, awkward teenager—a subject of amusement rather than love...

She quenched the small, sharp pain so quickly that she was able to reassure herself that she had not even felt it. That sort of pain had left her years ago, when she had faced up to the fact that to Simon she would always be his kid sister's playmate.

'Oh, for God's sake!'

The roughness in his voice jerked her out of her reverie, the rough brush of his fingertips against her skin as he turned her round and skilfully started to fasten the buttons, making her skin flutter with tension.

'I can do it myself!' In vain, she tried to push him away.

He was standing so close to her that she could see the pores in his skin, the dark pinpricks where his beard grew, the iris of his eyes.

She could almost feel the rise and fall of his chest as he breathed, smell the warm, musky male scent of his skin as it mingled with the freshness of his aftershave.

It was a disconcerting sensation—far too heady for ageing virgins, she mocked herself, trying to achieve a plateau of normality among the unfamiliar sensations storming her.

He reached the button that lodged against the swell of her breasts and she found she was holding her breath.

Was that why her skin seemed to flutter, or had Simon's fingers really trembled as he touched her? It was over and he was stepping back from her. A kind of madness overcame her, a backlash from all the years he had treated her as a naïve child, and to her horror, she heard herself saying tauntingly, 'Thanks, Simon, but if this is supposed to be a substitute for making love with Grant...'

She broke off as she realised what she was saying, too shocked to even think of registering Simon's reaction.

'Are you asking *me* to make love to you?'

There was no expression in his voice at all. No sign whatsoever of any desire for her, of any emotion at all, she realised, as she felt the hot wave of embarrassed colour flood her face.

'No, of course not!' her voice was thick with indignation and shame.

'Then cut out the provocative remarks, or you might find you've got more on your hands than you bargained for.'

All of a sudden her embarrassment gave way to anger. She hadn't asked him to get engaged to her; *she* wasn't the one who had got them into this mess; *she* hadn't invited him to break up her dinner date and bring her back here.

'I want to go home,' she said flatly, without expression.

'Switching roles again, Jenna? One minute the sophisticated woman of the world, the next the sulky little girl... One day you're going to have to make up your mind exactly what role you *really* want to play.'

His accusation stung, the more so because it had an undertone of truth to it, but he couldn't know how necessary it was for her to do so much roleplaying—how desperate she was to conceal the truth from him.

'You're not going anywhere until you and I have sorted a few things out. That guy tonight—how long have you known him?'

'You know he's one of our clients. We were having a business dinner,' Jenna told him defensively.

'Yes, it looked like it! If I hadn't appeared on the scene, right now you'd have been conducting your "business meeting" on his bed, most probably in the mission—'

'How dare you!' Jenna interrupted him furiously. 'What right have you got to interfere in my private life? It's no business of yours what I do or with whom?'

'Oh no? You're my fiancée, Jenna.'

'But that isn't real.'

'It's real so far as our families are concerned. The other man at my table tonight knows my father. He could quite easily have said something to him. Like I just said, our families think we are engaged, and when we join them in France they're not going to expect us to behave like a pair of strangers.'

'Exactly how are we supposed to behave, then?' Jenna demanded. Why on earth was it that when she argued with Simon she always lost? Because he *makes* you lose your temper, a small voice told her, but she brushed it aside, too intent on venting her wrath to listen to it. 'Your mother told me this morning that she was giving us separate rooms. Do you know how that made me feel?'

Simon looked blankly at her. The fact that she was pretty sure he was doing it deliberately only added fuel to the flames of her wrath.

'She obviously thinks we're already sleeping together,' she told him acidly. '*Your mother* believes that you and I are lovers...'

'So?' His eyebrows rose. 'What are you trying to tell me, Jenna? That you're adult enough to go to bed with a complete stranger, but you're not adult enough to accept the fact that my parents and your grandmother tacitly accept the fact that this is the nineteen-eighties and, while it may not be the way they did things, you and I as an established couple on the verge of marriage will be lovers? Rather an odd double standard to have, I would have thought.'

Jenna ground her teeth impotently, knowing she had laid her own trap.

'Look, Jenna, we're engaged. Of course people will think we're lovers… You must surely realise that?'

'We are *not* engaged!' she practically screamed the words at him. 'Oh, damn it all to hell!' She took in a deep, shaky breath of air that pressed her breasts against the cotton of his shirt. It smelled faintly of him, she realised in frustrated rage. Was there no way she could escape from him? He was like some sort of insidious poison, spreading through every part of her life.

'I thought the whole idea of our going on holiday together was to show our families how unsuited we are, so that they would accept the breaking off of this ridiculous pseudo-engagement…not to play the happy, delirious lovers.'

Her dress was still in Simon's hand, and no doubt still soaking wet, but she had had enough. She wasn't staying here any longer to argue with him. His conniving lawyer's mind would soon outmanoeuvre any arguments she flung at him.

She stepped forward, intent on retrieving her dress, and caught her toe on a ruck in the carpet.

As she pitched forward she gave a small cry of fright, and landed solidly against Simon's chest.

'You really must stop throwing yourself at me like this,' she heard him saying. His voice was muffled by her hair, and by the oxygen loss to his lungs as she had landed on him. One arm supported her back, the other her head. It made her feel oddly vulnerable and weak. Her father had died when she was a small child and she wasn't used to the comforting warmth of a masculine embrace. It made her feel weepy, for some unknown reason.

'If this is your way of convincing our folks that we aren't suited, I have to tell you that it isn't going to work... Look in the mirror.'

She could hear the laughter muffled in his voice, and reluctantly she turned her head and looked at their reflection in the full-length glass.

It would have been impossible to get so much as a feather between their bodies, she realised disgustedly, and she was clinging to Simon like a fainting heroine, her arms locked around him. How fragilely slender her arms and legs looked where they protruded from the depths of his shirt. How tall he was...she didn't have her shoes on...how broad, and somehow comfortable to lean on. How well his hand fitted into the small of her back.

She wriggled protestingly, disturbed by her thoughts, and to her horror she felt her nipples suddenly tighten in sexual arousal. She dared not move away from him. If she did, he would be bound to see. Panic flared inside her. It was just a physical reaction to the close proximity of a male, she knew that, but she couldn't bear the thought of Simon seeing, and perhaps...

'What's wrong? No fierce backchat? That's not like you.'

He was starting to release her. She shivered slightly.

'It's just the shock.'

Instantly he frowned, his hand withdrawing from her hair to cup her chin and tilt her face.

'Are you sure you're all right?'

His concern was completely genuine, and because of that it caught her off guard. She stared up at him through eyes which for no reason at all had decided to film with tears...

'Oh Jen, I'm sorry. I'm the one who got us both in this mess, but I...'

'Love to torment me,' Jenna supplied shakily for him. 'Sometimes I think you forget that I'm not fifteen any more.'

He gave her an odd look and seemed about to say something, and then, as though he had thought better of it, he said matter-of-factly, 'Are you OK now?'

'Yes, I'm fine.'

Well, it wasn't entirely a lie. At least she had her rebellious body back under control again.

As she started to step back from him, he lifted his hand to push her hair out of her eyes. She looked at him, offering a tentative smile.

'Friends?'

There was an unfamiliar huskiness to his voice; her own throat felt thick with tears, and so she nodded in response.

'Good.'

He tilted her chin, and before she realised what was happening his mouth touched hers.

It was only the merest brush of mouth against mouth, over almost before she had time to realise what was happening, but it left her prey to the most startling sensations. For a minute there she had not wanted him to let her go. She had wanted... She took a deep, shuddering breath to relieve her tension, deliberately avoiding meeting his eyes.

She had endured far too much emotion for one night, she told herself hardily. That was all that was wrong with her—an excess of emotion...

'Come on, I'll drive you home.'

'But my dress...'

'I'll drop it off tomorrow.'

She didn't argue with him. She was as anxious to get rid of him as he patently was of her, she told herself acidly as she followed him downstairs.

'Have you heard from Susie yet?'

He threw the question at her over his shoulder as they went downstairs, but Jenna immediately stiffened.

'No, I haven't, and even if I had—'

'You wouldn't tell me. OK, I'm not asking you to betray your ''best friend'',' he mocked her. 'But if she does get in touch, you might tell her that I've taken her point, and that if she's had enough of her fortune hunter, she's perfectly free to come home.'

'Do you really think that's why he wants to marry her?'

'I'm sure of it, but I'm also sure that my baby sister, despite her idiotic need to fling herself headlong into one dangerous situation after another, has the brains to realise for herself what the situation is... She won't marry him. I'm sure of that.'

He sounded so positive the Jenna didn't argue with him. She still felt hurt that Susie hadn't confided in her, that she had used her... How well did she know the girl she had always thought of as being so close to her, as though they were sisters? But then, did sisters always tell each other everything?

She was really too tired to dwell on the matter tonight... Tomorrow would be time enough.

Simon dropped her off outside her flat, and waited until she was safely inside before driving off. She heard the comforting roar of the Aston's engine as he drove away.

All in all it had been a distinctly odd kind of evening, especially for someone who was more used to spending her free time either alone in her flat pursuing one or other of her hobbies, or dining out with old friends like Craig and Susie.

Overnight her life had taken a dramatic turn in a fresh direction, and all because of Simon Townsend, or so it seemed.

CHAPTER FIVE

A WEEK before they were due to leave for the Dordogne, Jenna discovered that she was out of work.

Right from the start Rick had been opposed to her taking all her holiday allowance at the one time but, after the night she had had dinner with Grant Freeman, he became even more peevishly opposed to her holiday.

Not one single day passed without him making some comment or another about the inconvenience her holiday was going to cause him. Rick could be extremely virulent when the mood took him, and although Jenna knew that more than half of his acid remarks sprang from the fact that he was going through a bad patch businesswise, she was still beginning to resent the almost constant digs at her lack of loyalty and selfishness in wanting to take her holidays at what could be one of their busiest times.

She knew that it hadn't helped that she had practically walked out on Grant Freeman, although nothing had been said about that directly—until yesterday.

She had been ten minutes late back from her lunch—mainly because Rick had asked her to buy some special folders from their stationers, and she had had to wait almost half an hour for them to find them.

She wasn't in the best of moods herself; she had intended to spend her lunch hour shopping for holiday clothes, so she wasn't exactly pleased to be hauled over the coals by an infuriated Rick, in front of several other members of the staff.

'You realise that because of you we could lose the Freeman contract?' he had bawled at her, red-faced and furious.

In that moment Jenna's own temper had ignited and she had said angrily, 'If you lose that contract it will be nothing to do with me!'

'Don't be such a little fool... All you had to do was to be nice to him, butter him up a bit. And instead, what do you do, but produce some damn fiancé!' Rick had said in bitter disgust.

Initially Jenna had been too taken aback to say anything, and then, as the full import of his scathing remark hit her, she had started to tremble, so fierce was the surge of rage that swept her.

In front of almost half the office she retorted bitingly, 'I thought my job here was to work as your assistant, Rick, not to pander to the sexual needs of your clients.'

And with that she had picked up the coat she had just been in the act of putting down, gathered up her handbag and walked out.

In the circumstances she had hardly been surprised

to receive a telephone call from Rick later in the afternoon telling her that she need not come back.

She had already noted that he was a man who hung on to his anger, very clever and talented where his work was concerned, but inclined to be as sulky and vindictive as a child when things did not go his way.

She had told herself that it didn't really matter, and that there were always jobs for good secretaries, but even so nothing could quite banish the feeling of sick despair that swept over her.

Financially she was reasonably secure. She had her savings, and the small inheritance she had received from her parents on her twenty-first birthday. She knew that Gran would welcome her back at home with warmly comforting arms, but that was not the point. The point was that she had allowed the temper she had always rigorously denied she possessed to explode in such a way that Rick had had no other course but to apologise to her or to dismiss her.

Despite the fact that she knew her dismissal to be unfair, she was left with a lingering aftertaste of guilt and despair. The very last thing she felt like doing now was going on holiday. And it was all Simon's fault, every last bit of it.

On impulse she decided to go and spend the day with her grandmother. She would be travelling to France with Simon's parents, a few days ahead of Simon and herself, who were taking a mid-week ferry to avoid the weekend rush. She had intended to spend the day shopping, but somehow she didn't feel in the mood.

Had Susie been in London, she could have gone and cried on her shoulder, but, of course, she had no idea where her friend was, and Craig was away doing work for *Vogue*.

She knew she was being irrational and babyish, but that didn't help; she was running home to lick her wounds and be cosseted and wrapped in the security of her grandmother's affection.

As she drove north-west, Jenna's mouth curled in a wry smile. While her grandmother looked the part of the small, delicate, white-haired old lady, she was far from the fragile Edwardian figure she appeared.

For one thing, she had had a career in the days when it was almost unknown for women to work. Having been widowed early on in the Second World War, she had been left with a young daughter to bring up virtually on her own, and so she had had to go out to work.

Although it was now several years since she had retired and sold the exclusive dress shop she had owned and run in Gloucester, she was still a very active woman, participating in so many of the village activities that Jenna often wondered where she found her energy.

An ear infection as a child had left her with a hearing problem which had intensified recently, but apart from that she was very hardy, and never missed her daily walk of at least two or three miles.

When her parents had been killed, Jenna had found her a refuge and a comfort, and it was only since coming to adulthood herself that she had realised what a terrible blow it must have been to her grandmother to lose her only child.

They got on well together. Gran had encouraged her to read, to enjoy life in the countryside, setting her standards which, although some might find slightly old-fashioned, were ones Jenna would in time want to pass on to her children.

Harriet Soames was not the archetypal grandmother, longing for the day when her one grandchild married, but she had always liked Simon. She would be disappointed when their 'engagement' was broken off.

Subduing the small pang she herself felt as she dwelt on the reason for their coming holiday, Jenna pressed a little harder on the accelerator.

She had warned her grandmother to expect her around lunch time, and it was almost that now.

Nothing had changed in the village—nothing ever did.

The Vicar saw her driving down the main street and waved to her. Jenna waved back.

Her grandmother's cottage stood alone, set back from the roadside and surrounded by a stone wall, from which flowers tumbled in bright profusion.

It was built of Cotswold stone, under a thatched roof, and every time the thatch had to be removed, her grandmother threatened to replace it with slate. She never would, of course. Jenna knew that.

She parked her car and went in through the back gate. A lazy, fat ginger cat lay sunning himself by the doorstep, his purring deepening as Jenna approached. She bent down to scratch his ears before going inside.

'Is that you, Jenna?'

No one in Little Thornham locked their doors. It was a very small village, where everyone knew anyone else, and as Jenna called out a confirmation her grandmother walked into the room.

'Mm... You don't look very happy for a newly engaged girl. What's wrong?'

'I've lost my job.'

Gran's eyebrows rose a little.

'Well, you'd better sit down and tell me all about it. I've made chicken salad for lunch. Let's go through and eat.'

Her grandmother was a superb cook, and as she tucked into her homemade bread and farm butter Jenna acknowledged that nothing bought in any shop came anywhere near to comparing with their flavour.

Over lunch she told her grandmother a slightly edited version of her problems at work.

'And you've come all this way to cry on my shoulder?' she asked drily. 'Isn't that what you've got a fiancé for?'

She ought to have guessed that her grandmother would say something like that. Jenna tensed, and then said as casually as she could, 'Oh, Simon's very busy at the moment, getting ready for our holiday. I didn't want to add to his problems.'

'I agree it isn't a very pleasant thing to have happen, but it isn't the end of the world, is it?' came the practical response. 'After all, once you and Simon are married you would have had to give it up. I never realised when Bridge House was sold that Simon had bought it. Apparently, neither did his parents.'

Simon had bought Bridge House! Jenna stiffened. She knew the house in question very well indeed. It was barely ten years old and had been built by incomers to the village. It was a large house with well over an acre of garden, built in traditional Cotswold stone. What on earth had Simon bought it for? His business, his chambers—both were in London, but barristers could work from home, and weren't tied to normal nine-to-five hours. London wasn't that far away—not with a fast car like Simon's Aston Martin.

But surely somewhere like the village was far too quiet for a single man of Simon's age. Unless—she went cold suddenly. Had he genuinely intended to get married? To someone else? Was *she* the one who had caused that unmistakable look of anguish to darken his eyes?

It was a complete waste of time trying to fathom out the intricacies of Simon's emotional and physical entanglements, and not any of her business in any case, she told herself haughtily.

She came out of her thoughts to hear her grandmother commenting on the practicality of Bridge House as a family home.

'It's got five bedrooms, I believe, and two bathrooms, and that lovely big garden. Of course, Simon always did want a large family.'

Did he? Jenna hid her astonishment that he should have discussed such a subject with her grandmother.

'We aren't even married yet,' she reminded her weakly.

'Jenna, did you come all the way down here just to tell me you'd lost your job, or are you having second thoughts about this engagement? Simon's older than you and far, far more experienced. He already knows what he wants from life, but you...well, my dear, in many ways you're a very young twenty-four, and I don't mean that unkindly. I know when you were a teenager you had a crush on him, but don't mistake adulation for love, will you?'

Here was her get-out, so why wasn't she taking it? Why wasn't she telling her grandmother that it had all been a mistake?

Because of Simon's parents of course, but was it entirely that? she asked herself a little later as she headed back to the city. Was it just for the sake of her closest friend's parents that, instead of telling her grandmother the truth when given the opportunity to do so, she had instead vehemently reassured her that she was very, very deeply in love with Simon.

He rang her up that evening and didn't sound at

all sympathetic or repentant when she told him about her job.

'It had to happen sooner or later, Red,' he told her laconically. 'I shouldn't waste time getting upset about it if I were you.'

Before she could object to his cavalier manner of disposing of what was to her a very important subject, he went on to discuss the final arrangements for their holiday.

'I've booked our passage. Unfortunately, the only one I could get arrives in France at ten in the evening, so I've booked us into an hotel—it won't delay us that much and we'll have the advantage of getting off to an early start in the morning. I'll pick you up at, say, around three. We'll have dinner somewhere before we leave.'

He rang off before Jenna had a chance to question him about why he had bought Bridge House. Not that it was really any of her business, of course, but nevertheless, surely even bogus fiancées had some rights?

JENNA WAS READY and waiting when Simon arrived on the afternoon of their departure. She had elected to wear casual clothes for their journey, for comfort.

Like her, Simon was dressed in jeans; his were faded to an indeterminate colour between blue and grey, and shrunk almost to the point of indecency, she decided sourly as she glanced hurriedly away from the muscular tautness of his thighs.

He lifted her cases into the boot of his car with surely far more ease than was natural for a man of his sedentary habits, and she cast him a fretful, baleful look behind his back.

She had been in a bad mood almost from the moment of waking up. What on earth was she doing? The last thing she wanted to do was to go on holiday with him, but she couldn't get out of it now.

'Come on, Red. In you get.'

'Stop calling me that!' she demanded bitterly. 'You know how much I hate it.'

She heard him chuckle.

'It never fails does it, Jen? You always rise to the bait.'

It was a warm, sunny afternoon, and the hood of his car was down, folded beneath the cream leather cover.

There was no doubt about it, his car was far more comfortable than her own small Mini.

Just as they were about to set off, Craig emerged from his flat.

'Have a good time, and don't do anything I wouldn't do,' he cautioned her teasingly, bending to kiss her cheek. Out of the corner of her eye Jenna saw Simon's expression. All the amusement and humour had left his face. He was frowning, almost glaring at Craig.

'Idiot,' she heard him mutter as he drove off, deliberately obliterating Craig's 'goodbye'.

'As a matter of fact he's an extremely intelligent

and entertaining human being,' Jenna corrected him crisply. 'And he also happens to be a friend of mine.'

She saw the sideways look he gave her.

'A friend? Not so long ago you deliberately gave me the impression that you and he were lovers. Why, Jenna?'

She gulped, lost for an answer. The truth would be that she had reacted defensively, unable to bear the thought of him knowing the truth and teasing her for it.

'As I remember it, you were the one who suggested we were lovers... I just went along with it. After all, it isn't really any of your business whether we are or not, is it, Simon?'

He braked abruptly to avoid a cyclist with a death wish, and by the time Jenna had recovered her breath they were in such busy traffic that she deemed it wise to keep quiet.

Simon had allowed plenty of time for them to reach the restaurant where he had booked dinner. It was only a couple of miles outside Folkestone, where their ferry went from, but when they arrived they discovered that a group of people celebrating a twenty-first had virtually taken over the dining-room.

The manager was full of apologies and offered them a small table out of the way of the exuberant crowd, but it was in a narrow annexe which was used as a thoroughfare to and from the cloakrooms, and Jenna, sensing Simon's controlled and justified anger, was glad when the meal was over.

By mutual consent they didn't linger over it, and when they went outside Simon apologised to her for the mix up.

She found it rather touching that a man of his *savoir-faire* and experience should be so ruffled by what was, after all, an unavoidable error. She could have understood it better had she been a date he was hoping to impress, or a woman with whom he was deeply involved. As it was she made light of the incident, and reassured him that she had enjoyed her meal.

Even so, there was an odd air of tension about him as he re-started the car.

They were early for the ferry, and at Jenna's suggestion spent some time walking through the old part of the town behind the harbour.

The fishing boats were just coming in, and starting to offload their catches. Gulls wheeled and screeched overhead, squabbling frantically among themselves.

The air was sharp with the tang of salt and the smell of fish. At one point Simon put his arm round her waist to prevent her from being jostled by the crowd of onlookers—people like themselves, waiting for the ferry.

It felt good to be surrounded by a man's protective concern, Jenna acknowledged, leaning into him slightly.

'Time we were making a move.'

His voice came from somewhere in the direction of her ear, making her suddenly conscious of the fact that she was practically cuddling up to him. She disengaged herself hastily, hoping that he wouldn't guess the reason for the sudden colour tinging her skin. That was one of the curses of being a redhead: one's every emotion was so plainly visible.

CHAPTER SIX

'HELL!'

Jenna tensed as Simon suddenly swore and the car swerved to the side of the road.

'What is it?'

'Flat tyre.'

His voice was terse and uncommunicative—nothing to do with the unexpected mishap with the car—he had been like that almost from the moment they boarded the ferry. From before that moment, if she thought about it. In fact, she remembered the way Simon had disengaged himself from her as they stood watching the fishing boats, glad of the darkness to cover the embarrassment that recalling that incident brought. It reminded her acutely of her fifteen-year-old self.

'The spare's in the back. We'll have to take out all the luggage.' Luckily they were on a fairly minor road, and Jenna, who had had to change the tyre of her Mini on more than one occasion, was willing to give what help she could. Only Simon's Aston was a very different proposition from her Mini. The spare tyre, when finally they unearthed it, looked a good deal heavier than one of hers would have been, and

she found that she was holding her breath as Simon
jacked up the car and crawled underneath.

It took him some time to loosen the nuts and, to
judge from the occasional curses Jenna heard, it was
not the easiest of tasks.

Apart from themselves, the road was deserted; the
last village they had passed was miles back down the
road, and its single garage had been closed, but at
last Simon had the recalcitrant wheel free, and was
deftly replacing it with the spare.

Jenna wondered rather fearfully if the spanner he
was using would be sufficient to tighten up the new
wheel sufficiently, with nothing but mere muscle
power behind it.

As he emerged from underneath the car, Simon
saw her face. His own was smeared with grease, his
hair falling untidily over his forehead.

'Don't worry,' he told her. 'It isn't going to fall
off.'

Although Jenna denied that any such thought had
ever crossed her mind, she knew that she wasn't entirely convincing.

She was relieved that Simon kept to a relatively
slow speed when they set off again. His hands were
still smeared with grease and the smell of it mingled,
not entirely unpleasantly, with the scent of a physically active male body. She liked him better like this,
Jenna decided, glancing at him. He seemed more ap-
proachable, more human—less the barrister and more
the man.

Because of their hold-up with the car, they were later than Simon had anticipated in reaching the hotel they were booked into for the night.

Just outside a small village east of Toulouse, it looked practically deserted as they drove up to it. At one time it must have been a private house, obviously dating back quite some time, Jenna decided, noting the formal parterred gardens stretching to either side of the drive. Moonlight shadowed them silver and black and, as Simon stopped the car in the car park, she gave a final sigh of relief.

It always amazed her that travelling could be so tiring. It was somewhere round about midnight—not all that late, and yet she was exhausted, longing for her bed and a good night's sleep.

Simon had obviously stayed at the hotel before, because he knew exactly where to go as he took their overnight bags from the boot, locked the car and gestured to Jenna to follow him.

The main entrance to the hotel was some way from the car park, and when they got there the double doors were closed and locked. Simon rang the bell, and while they waited Jenna shivered slightly in the cool breeze.

Ivy covered what she could see of the outside of the building; she could hear it rustling in the wind.

The door opened, and silhouetted in the light from inside was a tall and rather imposing middle-aged woman, her dark hair confined in a bun. Simon addressed her in French, and the woman made an

equally rapid and, to Jenna, incomprehensible response. They were ushered inside with tuts of sympathy and understanding. *Madame* reached behind
the reception desk to a key and to say something
chidingly to Simon.

'What is she saying?' Jenna demanded to know,
weary beyond relief. For one moment out there she
had almost begun to fear that they wouldn't be let
in, and that they would have to spend the night sleeping in the car.

'She was just saying that we're lucky that she kept
our room for us,' Simon told her equably.

It took several seconds to sink in. Jenna stared
from his face to the single key he was holding in his
hand, and then croaked disbelievingly, 'What do you
mean? *Our* room?'

'WELL, LOOK at it this way,' Simon drawled, when
her temper had finally subsided, 'it won't exactly be
the first time we've shared a bed.'

Madame had left them to it, shrugging her shoulders over the incomprehensible way of *les Anglais*,
and they were still standing downstairs in the foyer,
from which Jenna had initially refused to move unless and until Simon got her a room of her own.

'Shared a bed? We won't be sharing a bed! The
bedroom will have two singles, hotels always do...'

'Well, in that case, I can't see what you're making
all this fuss about.'

'Oh, can't you?' Jenna was decidedly bitter. 'That

was how we got ourselves in this mess in the first place, wasn't it? Remember Mrs M?'

'Yes, but she's hardly likely to materialise here, is she?' Simon asked reasonably. 'And even if she did, we are engaged.'

He said it so virtuously that Jenna was robbed of breath.

'We are *not* engaged!' she practically screamed the words at him. 'And what's more, there is just no way that you and I are going to sleep in the same bedroom.'

There was an infinitesimal pause and then Simon said softly, 'Is this really the woman who was prepared to go to bed with a virtual stranger? What did he have that I don't, Jenna?'

It took several seconds for her to realise that he was talking about Grant Freeman.

She took another deep lungful of air to steady the quiver of anger shooting through her.

'I was *not* prepared to go to bed with him.' Suddenly she was exhausted—too exhausted to argue with him any longer, and what was the point? That adroit legal mind of his meant that whatever the argument was about he always won. 'Simon, I don't understand any of this,' she complained plaintively. 'Why is there only one room? You booked two.'

'There's obviously been a mistake,' he soothed. 'Look, we're both tired. Tomorrow you'll see the funny side of things. If it makes you feel any better,

I'll do the gentlemanly thing and stay down here until you're all tucked up and asleep.'

'The gentlemanly thing would be for you to stay down here, period,' Jenna told him acidly, but she didn't argue the point any further. She was exhausted almost to the extent of sleeping where she stood, and what was the point? Simon was hardly likely to take advantage of the fact that they were sharing a room to pounce on her... Heavens, five years, ten years ago, she'd have given her eye teeth for an opportunity like this. That restored a little of her equilibrium. What on earth was she getting so worked up about? She wasn't sure, but suspected that it had something to do with the fact that she was pretty sure that, had Simon been caught out in this situation with any other woman but her, he would have made full use of the opportunity fate had handed him. It was galling to admit that she stood in no danger of receiving any sexual advances from him. There, she had admitted the truth. Not that she wanted anything like that from him—no, of course not—but it would be very satisfying to be given the opportunity of slapping him down should he try.

Wearily she took the key from him and went upstairs. She found their room quite easily, unlocked the door, and put down her case on the bed.

The bed. There was only one, a very traditional French affair with a bolster and masses of pillows.

Off the bedroom was a bathroom, and she went

into it, too tired to care about the mix up in their sleeping arrangements any longer.

A warm bath made her feel slightly better. She pulled her nightdress out of her case and grimaced slightly. It was a brief affair of embroidered cotton and tiny satin ribbon straps. Susie had given it to her for her last birthday, together with its matching wrap. It wasn't the sort of thing she normally wore at all, and God alone knew what impulse had led to her packing it in her overnight case.

She creamed her skin, brushed her hair, discarded the wrap and climbed into bed. And it *was* a climb— the bed was several feet off the floor.

She removed the bolster and the extra pillows, turned on her side and almost immediately went to sleep.

Sunlight woke her, bright and harsh, reminding her that she had been too tired last night to close the curtains. She closed her eyes and turned over to block it out.

Next to her someone made a sleepy sound of approval, and an arm lodged firmly round her waist, trapping her. She opened her eyes. Simon was lying on his side, facing her, obviously fast asleep. She tried to wriggle free of his constraining arm, but it only tightened, his forehead furrowing as he made a protesting noise deep in his throat.

She was rather shocked to discover that she quite liked the sound of that possessive, instinctive male growl of ownership.

She yawned tiredly and closed her eyes. It obviously wasn't time to get up yet, and she might as well have half an hour's sleep. It did occur to her that by rights she ought to dislodge Simon's arm and get up and close the curtains, thus enabling her to go back to bed and turn her back on him, but she was far too warm and cosy where she was to do much more than muzzily acknowledge the thought.

The next time she was woken up it wasn't by the sun, but by the rhythmic caress of Simon's hand as he moved it against her breast.

He was still asleep, but his frown had changed to a smile and she could almost feel the contented purr of pleasure ripple through his body as his hand moved against her.

It was potentially the most embarrassing situation she had ever been in. It was obvious to her that Simon had no idea who she was; she was simply a warm female body in his bed, and he, like any other virile male animal, was reacting instinctively to the presence of a female. Much as she longed to push him away, if he woke up now...

If he woke up now, he would discover that her body was already responding to him, Jenna acknowledged. She didn't need to look down at herself to know that her nipples were pushing eagerly against the fine cotton of her nightdress, or that whenever his thumb brushed slowly over the tip of the breast he was caressing, it sent a spear of sensation rushing through her nerve-endings, that reached out to every single part of her.

At fifteen she had longed for this...spent hours and hours dreamily imagining what it would be like to be caressed by him, shivering in teenage sexual curiosity and awe at the power of her own emotions. But those idiotic day-dreams had long since faded.

She realised that Simon's thumb was returning more and more frequently to the aroused nub of her breast, and that his touch was far less tentative— much much more purposeful, in fact. How *could* he still be asleep? But he was. No doubt making love to a woman was so familiar to him that he could do it in his sleep, she thought wrathfully, trying gently to ease herself away.

It was the wrong move to make. For one thing it dislodged the tiny ribbon straps holding up her nightgown, and for another...for another...it had brought a frown to Simon's forehead, and a husky murmur of protest to his lips. He moved, his frown deepening as his fingers brushed against the cotton and then lifted away from her. Jenna held her breath, torn between relief and the beginnings of a not-to-be-acknowledged ache of deprivation, but then just as she started to ease herself away from him, Simon reached for her again. This time his touch was surer, more knowing, pushing aside the inadequate barrier of her nightdress, so that there was nothing to stop the tiny electric thrills of sensation running through her at the intimacy of their skin-to-skin contact.

He moved again, this time pinning her to the bed with the heavy weight of his thigh. His head rested momentarily against her breast, making her fear to even breathe and then, for the first time in her life, she felt the exquisite pang of pleasure thrill through her body at the touch of a man's mouth against the hardened centre of her breast.

It was so unexpected, so unanticipated, that she had no defences to block out what was happening to her.

She could only lie immobilised by the shock of the intensity of the sensations racking her as Simon nuzzled and sucked at the tender nub of flesh. His hand cupped her breast, moulding the soft shape of it, the muted sound of enjoyment he made deep in his throat causing Jenna to shudder under the assault of a fresh wave of sensation.

If he were to wake up now! Horror chilled her flesh, and as though she had somehow communicated her thoughts to him, he did wake up. She saw his eyelashes flutter, felt the sleep leave his body. He looked up at her, his hand covering her breast, almost as though in a way he was protecting her modesty.

He looked into her shocked eyes and swore savagely, releasing her and moving away.

'Jenna, I'm sorry...'

'I suppose you thought I was someone else,' Jenna said valiantly, and then added honestly, 'I was hoping that you wouldn't wake up...'

She flushed bright red as his eyebrows lifted and

she realised the interpretation he could put on her words, and hurried on. 'That was why I didn't wake you or push you away. I thought it might be embarrassing for both of us.'

'Embarrassing?' He laughed harshly. 'You surprise me, Jenna. I thought you knew too much about the male sex to make that mistake. Embarrassment is the last thing a man is likely to feel when he wakes up with the taste and feel of a woman in his mouth…'

There was nothing she could say. She felt vulnerable and raw, aching from a need she didn't want to acknowledge, frightened of the strength of the sensations he had aroused. And, most of all, uncomfortably aware of the fact that she hadn't wanted him to wake up because—because she had wanted him to go on making love to her, and now that he wasn't, her body was protesting at its deprivation.

'Isn't it time we were making tracks?' she suggested huskily, not wanting to pursue her own tormenting thoughts.

'I'm sorry, Jenna. I've only confirmed all your worst fears about me, haven't I? Would it help if I…'

'I think we should both forget the whole incident,' Jenna told him hastily. 'I'm not a fool, Simon. I know quite well it wasn't *me* you were making love to. I suppose you're so used to waking up with a woman next to you, that it's almost second nature to you to…'

'Are you sure it was only embarrassment that kept

you silent, Jenna?' All of a sudden his mood had changed, anger taking the place of his earlier contrition. 'Are you sure there wasn't a little bit of curiosity there as well? If you do want to know what I'm like as a lover, you don't have to be coy about it. Who knows, with a woman of your experience, I might learn a thing or two as well.' He saw her face and laughed harshly. 'Oh, come on, surely you don't think Susie kept it all to herself? I know all about those early days in London when the pair of you shared a flat... Almost a different man every night, wasn't it? I know that every time I rang up a different male voice answered the phone.'

Jenna stared at him... In a way, what he was saying was quite true, but Susie had been the one with a different boyfriend almost every night of the week, not her. Of course Susie probably would have told him that they were *her* boyfriends, especially if Simon had been about to go into his notorious 'big brother' act.

'Don't look at me like that. We both know I'm far from being the first man to find the taste of your breasts so intoxicating that I could almost forget how many men have enjoyed them—and you—before me.'

Jenna was almost lost for words. Why, it was almost as though Simon was jealous! 'You're being very old-fashioned in employing such an out-dated double standard, aren't you, Simon?' she asked when she had got her breath back. 'After all, you've scarcely been celibate, have you?'

'I may not have been celibate, but the women who had shared my bed have all meant something to me emotionally, Jenna. Can you say the same for the men who have shared yours?'

It would have been the easiest thing in the world to tell him the truth, but instead, for some perverse reason she snapped acidly, 'It's just as well we aren't engaged, Simon. And *as* we're not, my past, and the men in it, are my affair, wouldn't you say?'

THERE WAS still an atmosphere between them when they left the hotel. Jenna had remained stubbornly silent over breakfast, ignoring all Simon's acid comments about her 'sulks'.

She wasn't sulking; she was simply in no mood to want to talk to him. How dared he criticise her morals, her way of life? How dared he comment on her sex life?

She sat by his side, silently fuming as the miles sped by. The early promise of a good day had held, and when he stopped the car and asked if she had any objections if he put the hood down, she shook her head.

Mingled with her anger over their quarrel were other, more worrying emotions. She was dreading this coming holiday with their families…that was only natural, but what was worrying her even more was the intensity of this morning's physical response

to him. Even now, while she was still furious with
him, she had only to think of the way he had held
and caressed her for that dull ache to start up again
in the pit of her stomach and for her nipples to press
yearningly against the soft fabric of her bra. Luckily
she was wearing a loose, heavy cotton sweat-shirt
style top which concealed all signs of her body's
burgeoning arousal.

In other circumstances she would have enjoyed
their journey, but today she was still too caught up
in the complexities of emotions and worries that were
still unnervingly new to her to have time to spare for
the beauty of their surroundings.

Like her, Simon seemed disinclined to talk. They
stopped mid-morning and drank rich, dark coffee by
the roadside under the shade of some trees.

'Is it much further?'

She didn't look at Simon as she asked the question. Every time she did look at him she remembered
how she had felt when he... Confused and semi-
frightened, she pushed the unwanted memories aside.

'Another hour or so should do it.'

She had her first glimpse of the river itself once
they were past Calles, the rich pastoral French countryside spread out before them.

Simon's parents' farmhouse was off the beaten
track, several kilometres from a delightfully old-
fashioned riverside village built of red sandstone.
Jenna would have liked to stop and explore it, but

she sensed Simon's anxiety for their journey to be over with.

A narrow farm track led to the farmhouse, set among some of the most beautiful ancient trees Jenna had ever seen. The Aston took the track like the thoroughbred that it was, with scarcely a complaint. The farmhouse, long and low, squatted against its green background. White shutters broke up the uniformity of the stone, and an ancient wisteria curled along its frontage, its branches gnarled and nearly as grey as the stone itself. Parked to one side of the cobbled yard was Simon's parents' car. He stopped alongside it.

An odd sense that somehow she had reached a very momentous moment in her life took hold of Jenna, and wouldn't be shaken off. She remained where she was, unwilling to move, to face the moment when she would have to play the part of Simon's fiancée. But it wouldn't be for long, she reassured herself. It wouldn't be for long.

'Come on, let's go inside.'

She let him take her arm, her body and face stiff and tense. They found his parents and her grandmother sitting in the garden to the rear of the house. They were listening to Mozart on the radio, which explained why they had not heard them arrive.

'Goodness, you two have made good time!' Ellen Townsend announced, jumping up to fuss over and welcome them. 'We didn't expect you quite so soon. Are you hungry? You must be…'

'Sit down, Ma, and stop fussing,' Simon directed, bending down to kiss her.

'Jenna, my dear...' A fond hug and a bright-eyed smile said more than any words, and Jenna felt dreadfully guilty. She hated deceiving Simon's parents like this. They were kind, genuine people, who honestly thought of her as their daughter-in-law to be, and were prepared to welcome her to their family as such.

Simon's father gave her a slightly embarrassed hug, and greeted his son with a handshake.

Of them all only her own grandmother seemed at ease, affectionately kissing them both.

'Dear me,' she announced when she stood back from them. 'Have you two quarrelled?'

Simon's mother glanced in startled dismay from Simon's rigid back to Jenna's set face and murmured worriedly, 'Oh dear! Never mind, you'll soon make it up.'

Her concern only increased Jenna's feeling of guilt.

'It wasn't really a quarrel,' she said as reassuringly as she could. 'Just a little mutual grumpiness over breakfast. We had a puncture last night and were late getting to our hotel, weren't we, darling?'

Her tongue seemed to stick to the word, causing it to have a rather odd huskiness.

Simon turned and looked at her with an unfath-omable expression. Would he realise that the plead-

ing look she was giving him was for his parents'
benefit and not her own?

He walked towards her, and slid his hand caress-
ingly against the nape of her neck beneath her hair.

'Yes, you wouldn't believe how bad-tempered she
can be in the morning! Already I'm beginning to
have second thoughts about this engagement,' he
drawled teasingly.

Immediately everyone relaxed, and to show him
that she was just as good at putting up a front as he
was, Jenna grimaced mock-seriously, and gave a little pout, aiming a light punch at his chest.

Immediately he caught hold of her fingers, laugh-
ing at her; but what she hadn't expected was that he
would transfer them to his lips, slowly caressing
them, his eyes never leaving her face.

A flood of sensations assailed her, a feeling that
somehow the ground beneath her feet had become
less steady. She felt almost faint, and realised that
she was holding her breath. When she released it she
did so shakily, confused by what was happening to
her.

Behind her she heard Simon's father give a slight
cough.

'No need to eat the girl, Simon. Your mother's got
enough food here to feed an army.'

They all laughed, and the momentary sensation of
being so aware of him that she couldn't drag herself
away from his face faded and Jenna relaxed.

Over lunch the older members of the party discussed their holiday plans. The awkwardness Jenna had anticipated she might feel receded slightly. Although seated next to her, Simon had reverted to being the person she had always known, and not the stranger who had touched her so intensely both emotionally and physically this morning.

Jenna found that she was hungry, more than ready to eat the crusty French bread and homemade pâté with its accompaniment of crisp salad.

It appeared that Simon's parents and her grandmother had been invited to have dinner with a French couple Simon's parents knew—a lawyer and his wife.

'I don't suppose the pair of you will object too strenuously to being left on your own,' Simon's father teased.

Jenna could feel herself blushing and hated herself for it. She was supposed to be convincing them all that she and Simon were quite definitely not suited, not acting the part of the blushing, eager fiancée.

After lunch Simon and his father went for a walk, while the three women stayed in the garden.

Simon's mother was full of questions about the wedding—questions Jenna had no idea how to answer, and which Simon should have been there with her to field, Jenna fumed inwardly. Somehow or other, and she wasn't quite sure how it had happened, by the time the two men returned, she seemed to have agreed to a September wedding, with Simon's cousin's two little girls as bridesmaids, as well as

Susie, a marquee on the lawn and a three-tier cake, complete with a top tier that could be kept for the birth of their first child.

And the worst thing of all was that she felt a ridiculous temptation to just sit back and let herself be swept away by the entire fantasy… It would serve Simon right if she did, she thought irefully. After all, he was the one who had got them into this mess.

She got up pointedly when Simon and his father came back, and gave him a sweetly solicitous smile, saying to him, 'Come and sit down here, darling… Your mother and I were just discussing plans for the wedding. I'm afraid you're going to have to exercise that legal brain of yours and give us a decision worthy of Solomon. Who shall we have as our page boy? Your cousin Francine's son, or your godmother's daughter's?'

With another acid smile, she stalked past him, leaving him to it.

CHAPTER SEVEN

THINGS were not going as they had planned. They had been in France for a week now and, far from perceiving how ill-matched she and Simon were, his parents and to a lesser extent her own grandmother, seemed to think that they were the perfect couple.

Jenna found it unnerving. Not so much because she knew how wrong they were, but because she herself was actually slipping into the same trap. There were times when she actually *forgot* that she and Simon were not engaged. And he was as much to blame for this as their families.

Far from promoting the quarrels between them that were supposed to lead to their eventual breakup, Jenna was discovering that they had far more in common than she had ever supposed.

They seemed to feel the same way on so many major issues, and yet how could that be? She was liberal-minded and compassionate. Simon was altogether tougher and surely far more conservative, and yet when she had voiced her fears that in becoming the new owner of Bridge House he might do away with the beech hedges that surrounded the property, in which many birds nested, he had reassured her that he had no such intentions, betraying a sentimentality she had never suspected existed beneath his cynical exterior.

Of course, both their families were delighted that they would be living close at hand. As yet, Jenna had not figured out why Simon should buy himself such a large, family-style house, unless of course he looked upon it in the nature of an investment, or possibly a home for himself and his wife when he did eventually marry.

During the languid, sunny afternoons, if they were not out exploring the countryside, they sat by the river, watching the fish, talking in the desultory fashion warm weather brings. Sometimes Simon would discuss some of his cases with her, and unwillingly Jenna found herself becoming fascinated by the complexities of the law—complexities she had never known existed.

The matter of her own job, or rather the lack of it, was something she had pushed to the back of her mind. She would just have to keep her fingers crossed and hope that she would be able to find something.

'What will you do about your London house, Simon?' his mother asked him over tea one afternoon. 'Will you keep it or...?'

'Keep it, I think. It will make a handy *pied-à-terre* for those occasions when a court case keeps me in London overnight, and then later, no doubt, Jenna will want to come up to town shopping.'

'I do hope Susie's all right.' A faint frown marred Mrs Townsend's forehead. 'I've no idea where she's disappeared to this time… She rang me up and said something about going away on holiday with a friend.'

She didn't see the look Simon and Jenna exchanged.

'Anyway, she has a key to the house, and I've left her a note telling her how long we'll be here. Who'd have thought all those years ago when you and Susie became friends, that you and Simon would end up getting married.' She gave a romantic sigh. 'The two of you used to quarrel so much.'

'Ah, but Jenna loved me even then, didn't you, darling?'

The teasing note in Simon's voice made them all laugh—all of them but Jenna. She glared at him and moved her chair slightly away from him.

'I had an idiotic teenage crush on you, yes,' she agreed quellingly.

Diplomatically her grandmother changed the direction of the conversation by asking Simon's father how his delphiniums were doing.

George Townsend grew prize delphiniums of which he was extremely proud, and which he cosseted and worried over almost all year round.

As he launched into an explanation of the arrangements he had made for their care in his absence, Jenna excused herself and went inside.

Her room was right up in the eaves, and even

when the windows were open it was still hot and airless. She sat down on her bed and put her head in her hands.

Nothing was going as it should. Every day she and Simon were sucked deeper into their own web of deceit. And it wasn't just for their families' sakes that she dreaded telling them the truth, she admitted honestly. There was a part of her that didn't want to return to reality—a foolish, idiotically romantic part of her that wished it was all real, that she and Simon...

She got up abruptly and clumsily, trying to evade the thought, but it wouldn't go away.

She *loved* Simon. It hit her like a blow, making her wrap her arms round her body as she sought to control the pain flowering inside her. She wanted to deny her feelings, to dismiss them and pretend they did not exist, but it was too late.

The danger had always been there, and she recognised it now. Otherwise why had she worked so hard over the years to maintain her resentment and dislike of him? Wasn't it just because she had known how vulnerable she was? And now, because of the vulnerability...

'Jenna? Jenna, what's wrong? Are you in pain?'

Simon had followed her upstairs—no doubt still playing the role of the worried fiancé. She backed away from him instinctively, her eyes unknowingly shadowed and wild with anguish.

'What is it?'

She felt his warm breath against her temple as he reached for her shoulders, and she automatically ducked her head down so that he couldn't look at her.

'What's wrong?'

He gave her a little shake, much as he might have done when they were teenagers.

Anger spurted up inside her. 'What's wrong? How can you ask me that? Everything's wrong, Simon. Everything! We're down here to convince our families that it would be idiotic for us to get married, and all we seem to be doing is having exactly the opposite effect...'

'Maybe they know something we don't,' he suggested humorously. 'Perhaps we should forget *our* plans and go along with theirs.'

She went stiff beneath his hands. She knew he was only joking, but God, the pain of it!

'Jenna?' She heard the concern in his voice. 'Come on, I know it's a strain for you.'

Somehow her head was resting against his shoulder, his body taking the weight of hers. She felt as though she had come home after a long and wearisome journey. It would be bliss to simply relax and let Simon shoulder all her burdens, to turn to him and confess how she felt... Alarm signals prickled along her skin and she tensed again, frightened by how close she had come to a very dangerous dependence on him. She was letting herself be seduced by the myth of their engagement, because she wanted to believe it, she told herself miserably.

'Come on, things aren't really that bad, surely?'

She felt tears sting her eyes at his teasing sympathy.

'I hate lying to them like this.' It was only part of the truth—the only part she could tell him. 'We've got to tell them the truth.'

It wasn't what she had intended to say at all. If he agreed it would mean the end of her dreams. She felt him tense, as though he too shared her own despair, and then he said lightly, 'Let's leave things as they are for a little while longer, shall we? It will all work out in the end—you'll see.'

She thought she felt him brush a light kiss against her head, and she looked up at him, startled, her mouth slightly open. His grip on her arms tightened, his voice changing subtly as he whispered, 'You realise, don't you, that they all think we're up here making up? And I suspect if we stay here much longer, Ma will be here to chivvy us down. Jenna...'

She looked directly at him, her senses quivering under the rough note in his voice. She opened her mouth to speak and was silenced by the warm pressure of his lips against her own.

She struggled briefly to resist the desire rising inside her, and then gave up the battle, making a soft, inarticulate sound of pleasure in her throat as his mouth moved on her own.

She clung to him, everything else forgotten as she

gave in to the need that had stalked her for so long. The tenor of their kiss changed, deepening swiftly into passion.

'Simon, Jenna…'

The sound of Simon's mother's voice outside her door brought Jenna back to reality. She couldn't look at Simon as he released her. She felt too aware of what she might have betrayed to him.

'It's OK, Ma. We're on our way down,' Simon called out easily. He opened the door without looking at her, allowing Jenna to precede him through it.

All of them had been invited out to dinner by the same French friends that Simon's parents and her grandmother had dined with the first evening of their arrival.

The Le Bruns were apparently a sociable couple. Madame Le Brun had lived and worked in Paris prior to their marriage, and believed in working hard to prevent herself from becoming '*le cabbage*' as she described it to Jenna's grandmother.

They had two children, both of whom had now left home and who were studying in Paris, but, despite all that she had been told about the Le Bruns, Jenna was not looking forward to the evening, mainly because it involved taking their deception yet another stage forward.

She dressed for it reluctantly, and was still undecided about which of the two semi-formal dresses she had brought with her she should wear when her bedroom door opened and her grandmother came in.

As always Jenna was struck, not just by her grand-mother's femininity and elegance, but also by the energy which seemed to radiate from her. Although she had been devastated by the loss of her parents, her grandmother had more than filled the gap in her young life; she had been a shoulder to lean on, a wise counsellor, and an example of all that a woman could be. Harriet Soames was very much the author-ess of her own destiny, the living proof that a woman could not just survive, but also lead an extremely full and happy life without a man.

As a teenager she had asked her grandmother once why she had not married again, and had been told that it was simply because she doubted that she would ever find someone who matched up to her rose-hued memories of her young husband.

'At least that's what I tell myself, Jenna. The truth is probably that I've grown too independent, too fond of my own way of life to want to change it.'

'I can't decide which dress to wear,' Jenna told her, indicating the two hanging side by side on the rail.

'This one looks cool and pretty.' Her grandmother fingered the cotton fabric of the blue dress with the white spots. It had a sailor collar and buttons all the way down the back. It was very demure.

'Jenna, is something wrong?'

Immediately Jenna tensed, turning away defen-sively so that her grandmother couldn't see her face.

'No, of course not.' She felt much as she had as

a little girl when she had been caught out sneaking a jam tart.

'My dear, I'm not trying to pry, or to interfere in your life in any way...'

'But? I thought you were pleased about my engagement...'

'I like Simon, you know that, and I should have gone on liking him whatever his relationship to you, but it is not my likes and dislikes that are important here, but yours. Forgive me if I'm trespassing, but...' She broke off and asked quietly, 'Jenna, do you love him?'

Here at least was a question she could answer honestly.

'Yes. Yes, I do...'

'Well, you know that I'm not an advocate of love being the answer to all the world's ills. Simon is a good man, a strong man too, and you're a very strong woman, although I don't think you realise it yet.'

'Everything has happened rather quickly.'

That was true as well.

'Well, there's plenty of time...or is that the problem?' Harriet asked her shrewdly. 'Too much time together, and yet apart. I suspect Simon is a man with a very strong sexual drive. This holiday can't be easy for him...for either of you...'

Her grandmother had never minced words when it came to sex, and Jenna had never felt any embarrassment in discussing it with her. Over forty years separated their views on life, but her grandmother had always believed in speaking frankly and openly about her views on morality. To Jenna she had passed on her own maxim that it was more important to retain one's own self-respect than the sometimes dubious admiration of one's peers, and over the years Jenna had come to see the wisdom and truth of this statement.

'In fact, I'm surprised that Simon elected to spend so long down here with us. I suspect he's finding it…rather frustrating…'

Her eyebrows lifted slightly, inviting Jenna to confide in her if she wished, without pushing the issue.

'No, I don't think it's that. I think everything's happened so quickly between us that we're both still suffering slightly from shock. All those years of mutual dislike…'

Again the grey eyebrows rose, and this time the still dark blue eyes gleamed slightly. 'Oh, Jenna, come on. I might be your grandmother, but I still have eyes. *You* might have held on to your resentment, but Simon lost his a long time ago…'

A knock on the door interrupted their conversation.

'Time we were leaving,' Simon's father called out.

'I'll go down and tell them you're on your way…but remember, Jenna, this marriage must be something you're doing for yourself, not for anyone else. If you go through life burdening yourself with the responsibility of the emotions of other people,

you'll never be free to be yourself, and one day
you'll resent it.'

Food for thought indeed, Jenna acknowledged as
she pulled on her dress, but how could she explain
the truth? She couldn't.

The Le Bruns' house was just outside the village;
more of a small château in reality, whose vineyards
had been sold off many years before.

They approached it through a turreted gateway, in
the same crumbling sandstone as the village, the
drive climbing upwards, so that when Jenna looked
back she had an uninterrupted view of the river and
the land stretching away from it.

Trees lined the driveway, growing in almost Teu-
tonic rigidity. When she commented on this fact,
Simon laughed. 'As a matter of fact, only last night
Dad was saying that the château was owned at one
time by a German industrialist. He took possession
of it after the defeat of Napoleon, and then had to
sell it when he was disastrously unsuccessful with
the vines. Perhaps he was responsible for these trees.'

The gardens to the front of the château were laid
out in formal parterres with miniature box hedges
and red sandstone gravel paths.

The Le Bruns came out to welcome them as they
stopped the cars. Madeleine Le Brun was small and
slightly plump, her nails and make-up immaculate.
She was dressed elegantly in black and white, her
only jewellery a pair of huge pearl earrings, her dark
hair pulled back off her face in a smooth chignon.

Pierre Le Brun was tall and lean, and very distinguished-looking. He *looked* like a lawyer, Jenna decided, responding to his formal kiss of greeting.

'So this is the betrothed couple. How excited you must be,' Madeleine said to Simon's mother. 'I must confess I am looking forward to the day when our Marie-Claire gets married.'

She smiled slightly as her husband said something to her in French and explained, 'Pierre reminds me that she is as yet only eighteen, and that since she is studying to become a doctor it will be many years before she is ready to give up her independence. Of course it is different now... In my day one did not pursue a career after marriage—marriage *was* one's career. One had children and certain duties in connection with one's husband's business affairs.' She gave an entirely Gallic shrug and turned to lead them inside. 'I confess, I do feel a slight amount of envy for Marie-Claire, but then one cannot have everything, and the world of today is a far harsher place then it was when I was a girl. Much as I still love Paris, there are times when it seems alien, and yes, even frightening...'

Jenna listened half-heartedly as Simon's mother agreed with her, telling her her own doubts about the safety of certain London streets.

They were standing in a shadowy hall with a black and white lozenge-shaped tiled floor, and an immensely heavy carved stairway.

Dinner was a protracted and formal, but not entirely unenjoyable affair. They were not the only guests, four other people being present, also close friends of the Le Bruns, and Jenna was amused to witness Simon being treated very much as a 'young man'. He took it with good grace, she thought, watching him. In terms of experience and skill, as a barrister he must certainly rank ahead of Monsieur Le Brun, a country lawyer, but there was no evidence of this in Simon's conversation as he good-naturedly responded to the former's questions.

After dinner everyone retired to the drawing-room for coffee and delicious home-made chocolates. Simon stood behind Jenna's chair, and she was excruciatingly conscious of him, to the point where, when he leaned over her to pick up his own coffee cup, her skin shivered in awareness and instinctively she moved away from him.

She saw him frown, just catching the barely perceptible darkening of his eyes as he straightened up. It seemed incongruous that such a very small action on her part should have aroused such an extreme response, but she could see from the hard line of his mouth that she had angered him.

At eleven o'clock Madame Le Brun subtly indicated that it was time for her guests to leave.

Simon's father drove off first, leaving Jenna and Simon to follow. The strain of the constant pretence was taking its effect on Jenna, and they had gone several kilometres before she realised that Simon had turned off the main road, and moreover that he was slowing the car to a halt in a convenient lay-by.

'What…Simon, why are you stopping?' she demanded uncertainly. 'Everyone will wonder where… what we're doing.'

'No, they won't,' he told her equably, switching off the engine. 'On the contrary, I'm sure they'll think they know quite well what we're doing.'

He saw from the sudden change in expression that she had grasped his meaning. Anger flared in her eyes, her skin heating.

'Why did you flinch away from me like that after dinner?'

No preamble, no opportunity for her to pretend she didn't know what he meant, but what could she tell him? The truth was… The truth was that she had been so unbearably aware of him that it had either been flinch away or betray to everyone present, including Simon himself, just how she felt about him.

Fear made her defensive.

'What was I supposed to do?' she snapped. 'Fall into your arms with a sigh of rapture? We're supposed to be showing everyone that we're not suited, not acting the part of lovers who can't wait to fall into bed with one another.'

There was an infinitesimal pause and then he said coolly, 'I was simply picking up my coffee cup… If you think that that constitutes lover-like behaviour, I begin to wonder at the nature of the relationships in your past.'

It was said quietly, but it couldn't have shocked Jenna more had he shouted the words to the skies. He was so dangerously close to guessing the truth. Panic hit her and she lashed out blindly, not choosing her words, only knowing that she must somehow stop him from discovering it.

'How dare you call into question *my* sexuality, just because *you* don't arouse me? Is that what it is, Simon? The fact that I'm indifferent to you? Well, I'm sorry if you can't accept that fact. I realise I'm probably the first woman never to desire you to the point of lunacy, but...'

Her head jerked back as he re-started the car with a savage oath, pulling out so quickly that she almost lost her balance. She had never seen him react like this before, no matter what the provocation. The reality of how much she had angered him left her feeling shaky and weak. She was possessed by a craven and dangerous urge to tell him the truth, but she suppressed it ruthlessly.

Tears clogged the back of her throat and stung her eyes, and she tried to swallow them down. She couldn't endure much more of this emotional torture. Why couldn't Simon simply *tell* his parents that they had made a mistake?

When they got back, she escaped to her room on the pretext of having a headache. She thought she saw her grandmother glance thoughtfully at her, but if she was suspicious she didn't show it, merely saying placidly, 'You always did suffer in hot weather. That Celtic skin, I suppose.'

As though in punishment for her deceit she *did* wake up with an aching head, but she knew that it owed more to her sleepless night and churning emotions rather than any atmospheric pressure.

She dressed and went downstairs, feeling listless and out of sorts. Contrarily her mood was not improved by the information that Simon had driven into the nearest town to see if he could get his spare tyre repaired, and also to collect fresh supplies.

'I thought he might as well get them for us, as he was going in,' his mother explained. 'I don't mind doing the local shopping, but when it comes down to it French supermarkets are just as boring and stress-inducing as British ones. We're going to Gouffre-de-Padirac today—it's a trip we've been promising ourselves for ages.'

'Yes, you ghoulish creature,' Simon's father agreed. 'What do you think of a woman who complains all year long about the lack of sunshine, and then when she gets it prefers to spend several hours underground punting along a dark, icy river?'

Jenna laughed dutifully, declining an invitation to join them.

'I'm afraid I'm feeling rather lazy. I think I'll just spend the day sunbathing and watching the river.'

'Well, Simon shouldn't be too long. We probably won't be back until this evening, so don't worry about preparing any meals. George is taking your grandmother and me out for dinner this evening for a treat.'

They left half an hour later, and Jenna wasn't sorry to see them go. She went upstairs and changed into a brief bikini top and shorts.

There was a spot by the river which she loved; secluded, and shaded by trees, it was almost idyllic.

She found the huge paperback she had bought on the ferry—a historical family saga of a type that she loved, and, picking up a couple of apples and her sunglasses, headed for the river.

In no time at all she was thoroughly involved in her book—she had always found reading a marvellous antidote for a fit of the blues, but now, guiltily, she knew that she was deliberately using it as a form of escape...but why not? Surely anything that reduced her present stress level could only be of benefit. She was desperately afraid of betraying the truth, and each day that went past seemed to wind the coil of tension inside her a little tighter.

Simon hadn't returned by lunch time, and as she went inside to prepare herself a light salad and take refuge from the hot midday sun Jenna wondered if his tardiness was deliberate. The thought that he could be feeling the strain as much as she was herself was a novel one, but that could explain his totally out-of-character burst of temper last night.

After lunch she cooled down with a shower, donned fresh clothes and, after covering her skin with a protective sun cream, returned to the rover.

The sun had changed direction now, and threw dense shadows over the river. She found herself beginning to doze, a legacy from last night's loss of sleep.

A male voice woke her...not Simon's. This was far less assured, hesitant almost, and possessed of an unfamiliar accent.

She opened her eyes and looked upwards. A tall, lanky man stood looking down at her, his brown hair sunbleached at the ends. He had nice blue eyes and a rather hesitant smile.

'*Pardonnez-moi*,' he began in awkward French, '*mais*—'

'I'm English,' Jenna told him with a smile.

'Oh, great! Perhaps you can help me then. I seem to have got myself lost. I'm looking for a farmhouse that belongs to some friends of mine. I thought it was down here, but I must have gone wrong somewhere. I wonder if you know them.'

He gave her the name of Simon's parents, and she stood up, dusting down her shorts.

'You aren't lost. This is the right place. I'm Jenna—'

'Of course, I ought to have recognised you from Simon's description.' He grinned at her. 'I thought he must be exaggerating, but I see that he wasn't. I'm John Cameron. I don't know if he's mentioned me.'

He held out his hand to her and she shook it automatically. What one earth had Simon said about her? And, moreover, she would have expected John to have learned about her via Susie rather than Simon.

'Yes. He has.'

'I'm over here on business, and I thought I'd give myself a short holiday at the same time. I knew that Simon's folks would be down here...so I thought I'd invite myself to stay here for a few days. Susie and I had arranged—' He broke off and asked abruptly, 'Is Susie...?'

Anticipating his question, Jenna shook her head regretfully. 'No, I'm afraid she isn't here...'

So *this* was the man Simon was so keen for his sister to marry. She eyed him thoughtfully. Yes, he would make a good foil for Susie's vibrant butterfly personality. Behind his shyness she sensed a solid core of dependability, a stubborn determination to pursue what he wanted...witness his arrival here.

Oh, Susie, she thought wryly, you won't escape easily from this one.

'Well, then, do you expect her?' he persisted.

Again Jenna shook her head, softening the blow by adding, 'Of course, that doesn't mean that she might not just turn up—you know Susie...'

She wasn't going to tell him that by now Susie could well be married to someone else. She would let Simon deliver that blow.

'Are you hungry?' she asked instead.

'Oh, look, I don't want to put you to any trouble.'

'It's no trouble, I was about to make something

for myself. Everyone else is out, but they shouldn't be all that long. I was expecting Simon back ages ago.'

Only now, as she said it, did she realise how long and lonely the afternoon had been without him. If they had really been engaged, if they had really been in love, they could have passed this afternoon blissfully alone...

Shocked by the sensuality of her own thought patterns, she hurried towards the house.

She wondered if John Cameron had booked into an hotel, or if he was expecting to stay at the house. There were still two empty bedrooms.

It didn't take long to throw together a simple meal. They ate it outside on the patio, exchanging desultory conversation.

He didn't ask her what she was doing at the farmhouse and Jenna did not volunteer any explanation. Matters were complicated enough as they were without her adding yet another victim to the conspiracy.

She suddenly heard the familiar, throaty roar of Simon's car engine and for a moment felt totally unable to move. Colour surged up under her skin, and she felt as idiotic as a teenager, suddenly about to confront her idol.

She heard the car door slam, and it galvanised her into action. She stood up hastily, half losing her balance.

John Cameron gallantly came to her rescue, leaping to his feet, and steadying her.

He was just about to release her, as she thanked him shakily, when Simon came round the side of the house. 'Simon...'

She wondered if John, like her, saw the sudden hardening of his mouth as he paused, before acknowledging his friend's greeting.

In anyone else that faint narrowing of his eyes, the way he looked from her to John and back again, might be construed as burgeoning jealousy...the response of a very possessive lover in fact, to seeing his woman in the arms of someone else.

Dismissing the notion as pure fantasy, Jenna hung back slightly to allow the two men to greet one another, but to her surprise Simon virtually ignored John's outstretched hand, coming instead to her side and putting his arm round her.

'I'm sorry I was so long. Repairing the tyre took longer than I expected.' He was standing so close to her that she could smell his sweat. To her astonishment she found it dismayingly erotic, aching to turn into his body and press herself against him.

'John arrived an hour or so ago,' Jenna told him, fighting to appear calm and normal. 'He thought he'd got the wrong place when he only found me here...'

'Jenna and I are spending a month with both families prior to our wedding.'

Jenna blinked at the warning off tone in Simon's voice. He *couldn't* really think that John... He must be getting carried away with his self-imposed role, she decided wryly, pulling away from him.

'I'm sure the pair of you have a lot to talk about, so I'll leave you to it.'

She had never visualised Simon as a jealous lover, having only previously had a teenager's awe of his masculinity. It was strange to imagine him as vulnerable to his emotions as any other person in love. But of course he was not in love, and any jealousy he was showing was simply another bit of role-playing and nothing more.

Even so, she spent the rest of the afternoon in shameful self-indulgence lying on her bed, daydreaming that Simon *was* her lover, that he *was* jealous...

She got up when she heard Simon's father's car returning, her body aching tormentingly. Determinedly she refused to feel sorry for herself. It was her own fault, she should never have given in to such temptation...

She shivered slightly as she went downstairs, her mind still full of mental images of Simon's golden body, her senses still so finely turned that it was almost possible she could actually feel the sensation of it pressing against her own.

CHAPTER EIGHT

'I HOPE I'm not intruding.'

Jenna was sitting in her favourite spot by the river, knees drawn up, hands clasped loosely round them, watching the antics of a pair of water rats on the opposite bank.

At the sound of John's voice they disappeared. She shook her head and smiled up at him. A phlegmatic, calm, gentle man, John was an easy companion. Unlike Simon, he didn't cause her to suffer a constant seething cauldron of emotions.

'There's something about water, isn't there? I grew up in Ontario, almost right alongside the Lake. My father farmed...'

'Is that what you do?'

He shook his head as he sat down alongside her.

'No, I design and modify computers. My folks are dead now, but the three of us, myself, my brother and my sister still own the land, only now we've converted the lakeside into a holiday marina, with log cabins and a caravan park. My brother runs it, and I normally go up and help him during the summer.'

He had been smiling, but suddenly he frowned.

'It's a good life, but not what you'd call sophisticated. Ontario doesn't boast anything like London, although I love it.'

Without him saying so, Jenna knew that he was thinking of Susie.

He confirmed it, saying awkwardly, 'You and Susie have always been friends, haven't you?'

'For a long time, yes, although these days our lives have taken different paths.'

'You know that we...that Susie and I were engaged?' He said it abruptly, turning his head slightly away from her as though to conceal his pain.

'Yes...yes, I do. I'm sure she didn't mean to hurt you,' she added softly. 'She isn't like that...just giddy, and slightly thoughtless at times...'

'She's like a rainbow,' John said sombrely. 'Dazzling and radiant, but impossible to hold on to, to imprison.'

Her heart went out to him, but what could she say? She had absolutely no idea how Susie really felt about him. The fact that her friend hadn't even confided in that they had been engaged, the fact that she had deliberately misled and lied to her... Now it was her turn to look the other way.

'Both Susie and Simon are very charismatic.'

'Yes, Simon's a lucky man...to have found someone like you.' She didn't know what to say. She could hardly tell him that her engagement was built on even less firm foundations than his had been.

It was relaxing, sitting here talking to him. He was

the sort of man who grew on one, Jenna decided. The sort of man who could provide a comforting bulwark against the unpleasant harshness of life. The sort of man who made good husband and father material. She could just see him patiently explaining things to small children, answering their endless questions... It was a role she found difficult to visualise Simon in, and yet some day presumably he would marry and have children.

Perhaps he would leave them to the care of his wife and a nanny, while he rose higher and higher up the legal profession ladder.

Barristers did not have much time for family life. And yet, in almost direct contrast to that, he had bought himself a house. She frowned a little, bending her head, and absently watching the progress of a small beetle along a stalk of grass.

What was it that made people fall in love so ridiculously and unwantedly?

Take herself and John. They would have made an almost ideal couple. She sensed that they shared the same ideals, the same values, and yet much as she enjoyed his company, there was no spark there, none of that savage, bitter excitement that raced through her veins whenever she set eyes on Simon.

'You must be looking forward to going home.'

His quiet comment threw her off guard and she stared at him, wondering if she had said or done something that betrayed the truth, and then she realised that he was referring to their supposedly imminent wedding.

'I still can't quite believe it's all happening.' It seemed a fairly safe remark to make.

John smiled at her. 'I rather thought those would have been Simon's sentiments.' He qualified his statement by adding, 'When they were in Canada last year, Susie used to tease him about you...'

Susie had teased Simon about *her*! She felt as though she had just received a blow to her heart. She had guessed, of course, that her friend must have realised how she felt about him, but she had never expected Susie to betray her by discussing her feelings with Simon, by joking with him about them... But then she had been inclined to be blind where Susie was concerned, she realised bitterly, remembering how her friend had used and deceived her.

She was mulling over her shock and pain, when John continued wryly, 'I must admit I rather envied you, when I heard Susie saying that you had held Simon at an arm's length for years. I wondered how on earth you managed to do it. It struck me quite forcibly that if I was to do the same thing with Susie, she might not have left me.'

Jenna barely heard the last part of his conversation. It was obvious that John must have somehow got Susie's teasing comment mixed up, if he believed that *Simon* loved *her*.

'It's hell on earth loving someone who doesn't love you back,' he continued quietly. 'It's self-destructive, and a whole host of other emotions I don't even like to name, and yet there's nothing you can do about it.'

Jenna felt for him. She knew exactly what he meant. She reached out and covered his clenched hand with her own.

A shadow fell across them and Jenna looked up to see Simon frowning down on them.

'Ma sent me to tell you that lunch is ready.'

Jenna accepted the hand that John automatically held out to her as she scrambled to her feet. She walked ahead of the two men down the narrow footpath, assuming that since they were friends Simon would appreciate John's company more than he would hers, but to her surprise, when she turned to wait for them, she saw that they were walking singly, and that Simon was still frowning and tight-lipped.

Maybe he was feeling the strain of this bogus engagement as much as she was herself. Well, if so, it was his own fault.

All through lunch Jenna was aware that something had annoyed Simon. He barely spoke to either John or herself, limiting himself to monosyllabic responses when anyone addressed a direct comment to him.

In someone else she would have questioned his behaviour, wondering at its cause.

After lunch he got up and said abruptly to Jenna, 'I'm driving to Cordes this afternoon. I believe it's somewhere that shouldn't be missed. Do you want to come with me, or would you prefer to stay here with John?'

The last two words were added silkily after a slight pause, causing Jenna to stare up at him.

There was absolutely no movement in his face, nothing to indicate to her that his comment had been made because he might feel it had been expected of him, rather than because he was genuinely jealous.

He was a better actor than she had ever dreamed, she realised, and when she saw the look of concern that crossed his mother's face, she was so angry with him that she almost challenged him with his deceit.

'I'd love to see Cordes,' she said calmly instead. 'Can I have half an hour to get ready?'

She had read about the ancient hilltop town in her guide book, and she took the precaution of taking a shady hat and sunglasses with her, when she went downstairs.

John was sitting outside chatting to her grandmother.

'Simon said to tell you that he would wait in the car,' his mother informed her in a slightly flustered voice. She accompanied Jenna to the front door, where she touched her arm lightly. 'Jenna, don't be too cross with him. He's always been inclined to be slightly possessive. I thought he'd learned to control it, but I suppose when you're in love...'

'John is one of his closest friends.'

'Yes I know, but Simon's loved you for so long,

waited for you for so long, I suppose he won't feel
secure until you're actually married.'

Jenna could think of nothing to say. She had no
idea what on earth Simon had been saying to his
mother, but it had obviously convinced her that he
was quite desperately in love. Much as she longed to
call his bluff, she knew she could not.

Nothing was working out as she had expected.
Every day she was falling deeper and deeper in love
with him, every day she spent here added to the legacy of pain she would eventually inherit, and yet
there was nothing she could do about it.

She got into the car in silence, avoiding looking
at him as Simon started the engine.

The top was down and the cool breeze welcome.
They were driving along a road shaded by trees, but
once they started to climb out of them Simon stopped
the car, and stretching across her opened the glove
compartment and extracted a silk scarf.

'You'd better wear this,' he told her curtly. 'The
sun's hot, and I don't want you getting sunstroke.'

There was nothing remotely lover-like in the way
he spoke to her, and Jenna felt a contradictory impulse to argue with him, even though she knew what
he said made sense.

She took the scarf from him reluctantly, shivering
as their fingers touched. What was it about this man
alone that could inflame her in this way?

They were half-way to their destination before he
spoke again, turning to her abruptly and saying

curtly, 'Leave John alone, Jenna. He's been through a bad time, and he doesn't need you in his life to add to his troubles...'

So that was the reason for all this. It wasn't jealousy at all! Of course she had known that all along, but still it hurt to know that his concern and care were for John, that she merited nothing at all from him, despite all the years they had known one another...

'He just wanted someone to talk to.'

'Yes, I know, a shoulder to cry on, a soft body to comfort him in the aching loneliness of the night.' His voice grew rough. 'How you love to torment them and lead them on, Jenna! I hope they find it was worth it when they eventually get into your bed.'

Shock drove caution from her mind.

'None of them...' she began furiously, stopping abruptly as she realised what she had so nearly betrayed.

'None of them, what?'

'None of them has ever seemed to be disappointed,' she said sweetly.

They were starting to climb, and Simon pressed his foot down savagely, causing the car to leap forward, jolting her against the restraint of her seatbelt. She would have a bruise there in the morning, and she added it to the growing list of her grievances in what she already knew to be a pitiful attempt to convince herself that somehow she could make logic outweigh emotion, and stop loving him.

Cordes, impressive though it was, with its medieval buildings and narrow dusty streets, did not hold
Jenna's attention for long. She was aware of the
timelessness of the town, its history and its past
greatness, but these things only impinged briefly on
her consciousness.

The narrow streets were busy and every time
crowds jostled Simon against her, she felt her body's
reaction to him. It was ridiculous that she could be
so easily aroused here in the street, by the most casual of physical contacts, and yet it was happening.

Simon found a shady bar where they could sit out
of the heat and have a drink.

The lemonade Jenna ordered was icy cool and
fresh, and she sipped it eagerly. Here in the shade
she could take off her hat. She pushed her fingers
through her hair to brush it off her face, and found
that Simon was watching her with a peculiar intensity.

Her fingers stilled and, as though everything was
taking place in slow motion, she saw Simon reach
out and tuck an errant lock of hair behind her ear.

His fingers felt warm and hard against her skin,
sending a quiver of tiny vibrations racing over it. Her
body stilled, her pulses leaping in frantic excitement.

'Jenna...'

She held her breath and waited.

What was he going to say to her? What was causing this curious sensation of hope and expectancy to
burgeon inside her?

She only realised how idiotically foolish her hopes had been when he said curtly. 'Try not to spend too much time alone with John. *We're* supposed to be engaged, and much as you so obviously prefer his company...'

Disappointment and pain made her lash out at him.

'Have you brought me all this way to lecture me about John, Simon?' she demanded bitterly. 'When we came out here it was so that we could show our families how unsuited we are—remember?'

'John loves Susie.' He said it flatly, threateningly almost, his mouth a hard, tight line.

'But Susie isn't here, is she?' Jenna goaded. 'I'm not a child, Simon, and I won't be told who I can and can't have as a friend—or as a lover,' she added for good measure. 'I'm tired. I'd like to go back now, if the prosecuting counsel allows.'

He ignored her dig, and stood up, almost wearily, Jenna noticed with a sudden spasm of concern. For so long she had thought of him as inviolate and impregnable that she tended to forget that he *was* human.

As they walked back to the car, someone jostled her and she lost her balance. Instantly Simon's arm came round her, supporting her, protecting her, she thought hazily as she relaxed against it. She was trembling slightly and he drew her to one side of the busy street, frowning down at her.

'Are you hurt?'

Only by him, and she could scarcely tell him that!

'You're shaking.'

She *was* still trembling—that was the effect he had on her. His arm was still round her, supporting her against the solid warmth of his body. She ached to lean into him, to close her eyes and rest her head against his shoulder, to... With a tiny shudder she drew away.

'I'm all right. It was just the shock.'

Determinedly she freed herself and started to walk down the street, leaving him to catch up with her. When he did, he was frowning.

'All right, Jenna, you've made your point. You can't stand me touching you. I suppose if I'd been John...'

'But you're not, are you?'

They were quarrelling again, she realised abruptly, turning away from him to hide the sudden glitter of tears burning her throat and swimming in her eyes.

'I'd like to go back to the farm, Simon. I'm hot and tired.' And lonely and defeated, and aching with love and desire for him, but she could not tell him that.

The drive back was nearly as silent as the one there, but as they drew nearer to the farm, Jenna made a concerted effort to make stilted conversation.

Simon's mother looked rather disconcerted when they walked in.

'Oh, I thought you were going to be out for dinner.'

She looked questioningly at Simon, who replied briefly, 'Jenna wasn't feeling up to it. The heat...'

'Oh yes, of course...well, never mind. Perhaps another evening.'

JENNA FOUND that the tension that had gripped her all afternoon only abated over dinner when John talked to her about his life in Canada. It was a country she had always wanted to visit, and soon the two of them were engaged in conversation.

'A pleasant young man, that,' her grandmother commented afterwards, when she and Jenna were alone. She looked at her granddaughter shrewdly. 'But not for you, Jenna. He wouldn't be enough of a challenge.'

What could she say?

'I'm engaged to Simon—remember?' she said shakily, standing up.

She went to help Simon's mother, who was making coffee in the kitchen.

'Simon's in the study making a phone call. He won't be long.' She glanced worriedly at Jenna. 'Engagements can be such a trying time. I'm glad that you and Simon were sensible enough to opt for such a short one.'

Simon came in just as Jenna was pouring the coffee.

'Fancy a walk?' he asked her casually.

Mentally she pictured the two of them walking hand in hand through the warm, velvet darkness of the summer's evening, and then perversely shook her head. She was far too vulnerable to him to risk anything like that.

'No thanks,' she told him shortly. 'I'm rather tired. Too much sun, I suppose. I think I'll have an early night.'

She didn't sleep well, her slumbers punctuated by odd, confusing dreams in which Simon featured heavily, but when she woke up in the morning she couldn't remember the details, only the tremendous feeling of pain and loss they had evoked. They had also left her with a headache.

The day seemed to drag. She purposefully kept out of both Simon and John's ways, but in the afternoon when she came downstairs from her room John waylaid her in the shadowy darkness of the hall, his face puckered in an expression of concern.

'Look, if I've caused any problems between you and Simon.... Would you like me to have a word with him? Explain that you were simply taking pity on me, commiserating with me, and letting me bore on about Susie?'

Jenna shook her head.

'There isn't really any need.'

'He always was oddly vulnerable where his emotions were concerned, and he's waited for you so long that he's bound to feel possessive.'

Jenna opened her mouth to tell him how wrong he was, and then closed it again.

The turbulence of her own emotions, the heat, the

total unreality of the situation she was in had combined to produce a kind of inner lethargy that refused to let her submit to anything that involved any kind of effort, either physical or emotional.

'Jenna.'

The sharpness of Simon's voice made her tense.

'I was just coming.' She stepped past John. At his mother's insistence she and Simon were spending the afternoon alone. There had been no way she could get out of it. The others were all going out, and taking John with them.

This morning over breakfast, he had announced that he mustn't impose on them any longer. Soon he would be leaving... Maybe then she and Simon could get on with the business of convincing everyone that they were not cut out to be marriage partners.

As soon as the others had gone Jenna got up from the garden chair she was sitting in. 'I think I'll go upstairs and lie down. I'm still feeling rather tired.'

As she made to walk past him, Simon's hand shot out, his fingers imprisoning her wrist.

'Oh no, you don't,' he told her angrily. 'What is it about me that's so repulsive, Jenna? What is it that I lack? You go out of your way to avoid coming anywhere near me, like a fastidious little cat. Do you do it to be deliberately provocative, I wonder? Or is it genuine?'

'Do you really need to ask?' Her voice shook and so did her body. She hadn't expected him to touch her and had been ill prepared for it. He was right, she did try to avoid any contact with him, and thank God he didn't realise why. 'You're forgetting,' she told him acidly, 'that you and I have never got on. I'm not the actor you are, Simon. This whole thing is a strain. We've been here three weeks now and we're no closer to breaking this charade of an engagement...'

'Is that what you want...to break it? So that you can be comforted by John? He doesn't love you, Jenna,' he told her cruelly. 'He loves Susie and he always will.'

'I'm sure you're right,' she said, with all the polite disinterest she might have accorded a stranger, still trying to tug her wrist free. 'Let me go, Simon!' She was getting angry now, angry and vulnerable.

'What if I don't want to?'

It gave her an odd swimming sensation in her head to look down into his face. His mouth drew her gaze like a magnet, her own lips parting slightly as she felt the coil of sensation tighten inside her.

She shivered, her eyes glazing with emotion. She loved him so much, too much... She tensed and tried to pull away, biting back a gasp as his grip tightened.

'What is it about me that revolts you so much? You look like a virgin facing the prospect of rape,' he told her harshly, his face contorting with an anger she couldn't understand.

'Jenna.' He was tugging her down towards him. She felt her heart slam against the wall of her ribs, her resistance and her grip of reality fading.

Another moment and he would kiss her... She could feel her inside churning at the thought.

'Break it up, you two... I'm too young and innocent for this.'

Jenna was shocked into immobility.

Susie! What was *Susie* doing here?

She felt Simon release her and stand up.

'The wanderer returns,' he drawled, going forward to greet his sister. 'And just in the nick of time by the look of things.'

As Jenna looked on in shock, brother and sister exchanged a look she couldn't understand.

'Where's everyone else?'

'Out sightseeing... John arrived here the other evening, by the way.'

Again there was an odd pause, a studied peculiarity about the way Simon delivered the information that made Jenna stare at him.

As she looked from brother to sister, she wondered what had happened to the rage and resentment Susie had evinced the last time she had seen her. And where was her latest conquest? She looked discreetly at her left hand...no wedding ring.

'Er—what happened to Peter?' she ventured to ask.

'Oh, it didn't work out,' Susie told her carelessly. 'We weren't suited.'

Jenna was lost for words. So much emotional anger over the man, and now he was so easily dismissed, but then that was Susie all over.

'I feel very hot and sticky. I think I'll go and have a shower. Why don't you come with me and we can catch up on our news?' Jenna suggested casually. She wanted to find out exactly what had happened after Susie had left her flat that day, and to warn her about her own extraordinary situation.

'No. I think I'll stay down here, and make sure that Simon behaves himself and doesn't follow you. It's just as well the two of you are only having a short engagement,' she giggled. 'From what I know of it, my dearest brother isn't renowned for his celibacy.'

Jenna stared at her. How did Susie know they were engaged? And what did she mean by implying that their engagement was actually real?

'Susie…'

'Look, I'm dying for a drink. You go and have your shower, Jen. We can chat later.'

Why did she have the impression that Susie was trying to avoid being alone with her?

'How did you know about our engagement?' she asked suspiciously.

Jenna didn't miss the flustered look Susie gave her brother. 'Ma left you a note, didn't she?' Simon interjected.

'Oh, yes. Yes, she did…'

'I see…' But she didn't and she was hurt that Susie was holding her at a distance.

'You go and have your shower,' Simon told her.

'I'll put Susie properly in the picture while you're gone.'

For some reason Jenna delayed going back downstairs. There had been an open degree of complicity in the look Susie and Simon had exchanged, a oneness that had excluded her and left her feeling raw and hurt. She didn't want to go back down to them.

She lingered until she heard the others return, and then quietly insinuated herself into a chair slightly away from them.

'I gather Susie's arrival wasn't entirely expected.' John's quiet voice held a tinge of irony.

'Not by me,' Jenna agreed, quickly frowning when she realised how hard it must be for John to see her. She reached out to touch his hand, wanting to comfort and reassure him, and at that moment Susie turned her head.

Anger flashed openly in her eyes as she looked at them. Jenna dropped John's hand as though it were a hot coal.

She had had enough of this, she decided bitterly. She was going to find out exactly what was going on.

Only Susie managed to avoid her right until they all sat down for dinner. It was frustrating to sit almost opposite her friend, and yet not be able to question her as she wished.

Susie was even behaving a little coolly towards her, most of her attention concentrated on her parents and Simon, while she and John were virtually ignored. She could understand why Susie might want to avoid any embarrassing conversation with her ex-fiancé, but *she* was virtually her best friend—had lied and covered for her with the direst of consequences, and now she was being treated as though she had broken the eleventh commandment.

Jenna tried to concentrate on her food. Susie was chatting eagerly to her mother.

'Such a lovely surprise,' she heard Simon's mother saying bemusedly.

'Well, yes, but when Simon rang me and told me what a wonderful time you were all having...'

Simon had rung Susie? Jenna stared at her, and as though suddenly aware of her slip, Susie hurried into a garbled tale about the holiday she should have taken with her friends which had fallen through.

She waited until dinner was over and Susie had slipped upstairs, and then she followed her, walking into her room after the briefest of knocks.

'Oh, Jen...'

Susie sounded awkward and unsure of herself.

'Did Simon ask you to come down here?' Jenna wasn't sure what made her ask the question, just some deep instinct she felt impelled to obey.

For a moment she thought Susie wouldn't reply, and then to her astonishment her friend said defensively, 'Yes, he did. He warned me that unless I did I was likely to lose John.'

'Lose John?' Jenna stared at her. 'But *you* were the one who broke the engagement...'

'It wasn't like that. We had a quarrel. I can't remember what it was about. I said if he felt like that he could take back his ring. I never expected that he would. It was just—it was just a silly quarrel. I love him, Jen.'

Jenna sat down on her bed.

'Then why all that business about Simon trying to force you to marry his friend... Why?' She made a hopeless gesture with her hands, unable to find the words to describe her sense of disbelief.

'Because I was angry, that was why... I knew Simon would find out what I'd done. I thought he'd tell John, and that John—'

'Would come running after you,' Jenna supplied grimly. 'Dear heaven, does Simon know any of this?'

'He does now. When he rang me last night and told me what was happening down here...'

'Nothing's happening!' Jenna told her, exasperated. 'At least, not between me and John. Susie, use your brains. I like John, he's a very nice man...ideal for you, you feather-headed creature, but far too stoical for me.' She got up and paced over to the window.

'What I can't understand is why on earth Simon would do a thing like that. He must be as aware as me that John is still deeply in love with you...that all he wanted from me was someone to talk to... Why? Why?'

She turned round and saw that Susie was looking oddly at her.

'Don't you know why?'

Jenna shook her head.

'No. No, I don't... Do you?'

There was a long pause, and when she did answer, Susie was rather evasive. 'If you really want to know, why don't you ask Simon? After all, he *is* your fiancé.'

'Oh, come on, you know how that happened!'

'But that doesn't make your engagement any less real, does it?'

Susie was employing a brand of logic that Jenna couldn't understand.

'We're supposed to be spending our time down here convincing your parents and my grandmother how unsuited we are,' she said fretfully. 'Instead of which, Simon's started acting like a jealous lover in a bad melodrama.'

'Maybe he isn't acting,' Susie suggested.

Jenna was lost for words.

'You can't be suggesting that...that he's got so caught up in this wretched fake engagement that he actually believes he should be jealous of John, are you?' When Susie made no response, Jenna gave her an exasperated look. 'Oh no, Susie, that won't wash. You know how Simon feels about me. God, it was plain enough when I had that idiotic crush on him.'

'That was nearly ten years ago.'

'Exactly, and believe me, nothing's changed, apart from the fact that I've grown up and realised that what I mistook for love was nothing more than a teenager's infatuation.'

A strange expression crossed Susie's face, but before Jenna had time to comment on it, Susie's mother knocked on the door.

'I'm sorry to interrupt, but Susie darling, what are we going to do with that very nice young man? He's making polite noises about leaving now that you've arrived…'

'Don't worry about it, Ma. I'll sort it out. The only way he's leaving is with me.'

'Simon's phone call brought one thing home to me,' Susie told Jenna, when her mother had left. 'Pride means nothing, when retaining it means losing the man you love. I'm going to tell John what a fool I've been, so keep your fingers crossed for me, Jen, and pray that he takes me back…'

CHAPTER NINE

HE DID, of course, and, to judge from the fatuously blissful expression on his face when the pair of them returned from their walk, he was as pleased with the outcome as Susie.

Jenna tried hard not to feel envious of her friend, but it was very difficult.

She felt apart and outside the excitement generated by Susie's announcement that they were going to get married just as soon as it could be arranged.

'Beaten you to it, brother, dear,' Susie teased Simon, ignoring her mother's wail of distress.

'John has to go back to Canada soon, Ma, and this time I'm going back with him—as his wife. We'll get married in church, but very quietly and quickly. And then all of you can come over and spend Christmas in Canada with us.'

This was a new, decisive side of her friend that Jenna had rarely seen before. She hugged her and wished them both well, but inside she was aching with loneliness and pain. She knew Susie meant nothing unkind by it, but to hear her teasing Simon about their marriage, when she *knew* that their engagement was only a sham, hurt her unbearably.

She was relieved when her grandmother diplo-matically said that all the excitement had left her feeling rather tired, and that she rather felt she would have an early night, because it gave her an excuse to go upstairs with her.

'Quite a surprise, Susie turning up like that,' her grandmother commented as they walked upstairs. 'I wonder what made Simon phone her.'

Jenna shrugged and tried to sound uninterested.

'I don't know.'

It was, after all, the truth. She couldn't believe that Simon had actually thought that John was in danger of falling out of love with Susie and in love with her—he wasn't the type. And yet, what other inter-pretation could she put on his hasty phone call to England?

For most of the following day Susie and John were busy on the telephone making arrangements for their wedding.

A phone call to their local vicar confirmed that they could be married after a minimum wait of three weeks. A date was set, John rang his family in Can-ada, all of whom were insisting on flying over for the event, and Jenna suspected that before they were finished Susie and John would find that their 'quiet, quick ceremony' had escalated into a full-blown af-fair.

The newly engaged couple were flying back to En-gland on an evening flight, and Susie had managed to persuade her mother that there was no necessity for her to return home immediately.

Susie and John left after lunch. With them gone the atmosphere at the farmhouse seemed less electric, more subdued.

Surely now, with the excitement of Susie's wedding to look forward to, it would be easier for Simon and herself to break their engagement. She wanted to suggest as much to him, but he had become very withdrawn, elusive almost.

No doubt he was tired of her company and looking forward to his return to London, and the sophistication of women of a far different type than herself.

Simon's mother wandered into the garden, where Jenna was sitting, worrying. As she sat down, Jenna noticed her frowning and touching her hand to her side.

'Is something wrong?'

'Just a twinge of pain—probably that quiche we had for lunch, it was very rich. I'm so relieved that Susie's finally settling down, and John is just right for her.' They chatted idly for several minutes, but after a while Simon's mother got up again, still massaging her side.

'I think I'll go and lie down for a while, Jenna… I really shouldn't have eaten that quiche.'

Her grandmother and Simon's father, who were both history buffs, had gone into the local town, at the invitation of Monsieur Le Brun, to look at its historical records. In a way Jenna wished she had gone with them. It would have given her something to think about, other than Simon.

She didn't even know where he was. He had gone out after lunch saying that he needed petrol, and he hadn't come back.

The day had been particularly hot, almost oppressively so, and she instinctively sought out her favourite shaded spot by the river, dropping down on to the grass.

She had brought a book with her, but she couldn't concentrate. She had not slept well for the last few nights, and when she found the print blurring in front of her eyes for the third or fourth time she gave up the impossible task of trying to occupy her mind with something other than Simon, and lay down, closing her eyes.

Even in her thoughts there was no escape from him. This holiday, which should have destroyed the last remnants of her childhood feelings had instead brought them back to life, but in a far more adult form.

Had she ever really stopped loving him? She knew the answer. Hadn't she subconsciously always compared every man she had dated with him, using him as a measuring stick, and finding others wanting? She twisted restlessly, bruising the grass and releasing its clean, green scent.

As a teenager she had cherished rosy vague dreams about him. Fantasies in which he had declared his love for her, kissed her reverently; now her fantasies had taken on a more earthy, adult quality.

She ached for the touch of his hands on her body, for the male reality of his flesh against her own. She shivered involuntarily, banishing the disturbing images that filled her mind.

The mid-afternoon heat penetrated even the quiet shade of her refuge. Her eyelids grew heavy, as sleep claimed her.

SHE WOKE UP abruptly, tensing with shock when she saw Simon leaning over her. His hands were on the ground on either side of her head, his mouth only inches from her own. Her lips tingled, almost as though he had actually caressed them, and she couldn't resist touching them with the tip of her tongue as though seeking his taste.

She saw his eyes change, darkening, desire flaring in their depths. It was a moment out of time.

His response to her was so unexpected that immediately she rushed into protective nervous conversation, demanding huskily, 'What time is it? Is it late? I fell asleep...'

'And I woke you—in the traditional manner,' Simon told her, his glance focused on her mouth.

She had been right; he had kissed her. Her stomach lurched in a wave of need. She wanted to reach up and urge his dark head down towards her. She wanted to touch him, to explore the tanned flesh of his chest, where his casual shirt revealed it to her eager eyes.

'Simon.'

He heard the tremor in her voice and smiled mirthlessly. 'What's wrong? Disappointed that I'm not John?'

She stared at him, her eyes widening as her breath locked in her throat.

'Not denying it? That's my honest Jenna.' He sounded bitter. 'You look surprised. Why, I wonder? Aren't I allowed to be resentful of the fact that you desire him and not me? We're both adults, after all, both used to living completely full lives.'

What was he telling her? That he was sexually frustrated and that he wanted *her*? She stared at him again, unable to believe she was right.

'John was only telling me how he felt about Susie. There was never anything sexual between us. You can't think there was?'

Simon gave her an oddly bitter smile.

'Men are inclined to think all sorts of peculiar things when they have a physical need for a woman who doesn't share that need.'

She waited for a moment, hardly daring to put her thoughts into words and then acknowledging that she must. 'Are you...are you trying to tell me that you want me...in a physical sense?' Try as she might, she couldn't keep the astonishment out of her voice.

'Amazing, isn't it?' Simon agreed self-mockingly. 'Definitely a case of how the mighty are fallen, but you aren't fifteen any more and we're meeting as equals now, Jenna...in knowledge and experience...not as innocent teenager and young adult male.'

'You make it sound almost as though before...as though it was for my sake that you...'

'Didn't take advantage of your feelings for me?' Simon supplied tautly for her. 'Is that so impossible to believe?' His hand cupped her face, the shock of the physical contact burning through her skin.

'How could I have seduced my sister's best friend...a little girl really, because that's what you were...and that's what it would have been. Do you remember that day when you saw me kissing Elena?'

Jenna nodded her head, her mouth dry.

'Well, I looked at you then and wondered what it would feel like to have your mouth under mine, your body beneath my hands...' He broke off and made a noise deep in his throat, a combination of despair and self-disgust.

'I still want to know. I've wanted to know for years. Imagine what it's like for me, hearing from Susie about each man in your life.'

'So I'm sort of the one who got away, and the challenge is still there like a itch, is that it?' Jenna asked faintly.

Inside she felt as though she was bleeding to death. To know that he wanted her physically but didn't love her; it was the very worst kind of pain.

'I suppose I ought to be flattered,' she told him

emptily. 'But I'm not. To be desired without being loved isn't flattering...'

'Are you trying to tell me you've loved all the others?'

He was openly scornful now, and for a moment she hated him, and then suddenly she was too exhausted for any further pretence. The shock of discovering that he had wanted her physically for so long had destroyed her defences completely.

'What others?' she asked him painfully, looking directly into his eyes as she added, 'There haven't been any "others", Simon, and before you say anything, there isn't going to be any "you". You can blame me, or blame my upbringing, I don't really care. Perhaps it's old-fashioned and out of date, but for me sex *must* be allied to love.'

She saw and felt the shock course through him, and then an expression she could only define as pity filled his eyes.

Instantly she tensed against the pain of it, knowing she was facing now what she had always dreaded facing: being exposed and vulnerable to him, an object of pity, a woman who had never known a man's desire, never shared the physical pleasures he had known.

'Don't feel sorry for me. Don't pity me because I don't have your experience,' she told him huskily. 'I...'

She didn't get any further. His mouth came down

on hers with a kind of mute savagery she had never expected to see in a sophisticated man like Simon.

His teeth ground into her lower lip, bruising it, his tongue claiming the intimacy of her mouth. Against her will she felt herself responding to him, something elemental in her blood responding blindly to the suppressed need of his kiss.

It was sheer physical desire and nothing else, but that didn't stop her body filling with a physical ecstasy she had never known could exist. She was completely lost, completely submerged by the tidal wave of need that swept her. Somewhere on the periphery of her awareness she knew that Simon had released her mouth, that he was trying to say something to her, but she wasn't listening. All her energy was consumed by the need to satisfy the ache inside her. She reached up and locked her hands behind his neck, wanting the sensation of his mouth against hers so much that she felt she would die without it.

'Do you honestly think this is feeling sorry for you?' Simon demanded, his tongue-tip running avidly over the swollen contours of her mouth. 'Or this?'

His words brought her back to sanity. She tried to turn her head away, to reject her own need as well as his, but he simply cupped her head and turned it back, plundering the set line of her mouth with his tongue and teeth until she could not fight against him any more.

The full weight of his body pressed her against the

earth and she welcomed it eagerly, greedily almost, like a miser hoarding up gold. She would cherish these moments, store them up.

'Jenna!'

She felt the shudder he stifled against her mouth, her whole body reacting to the sensation of his hand against her breast. He moved, lifting away from her, turning her so that he could unfasten her top.

It knotted to reveal her midriff, and beneath it she was bare.

She felt the air leave her lungs as his hands cupped her breasts. His lips touched her ear.

'Is this the first time?'

She shivered violently in response, unable to make any comment, but her very silence seemed to give him his answer.

Her skin seemed to know his touch already, eager to respond to it, her nipples swollen to aroused nubs of flesh.

The slightly rough friction of his thumb pad against such sensitised flesh was so exquisitely pleasurable that she couldn't restrain herself from crying out, her body twisting sinuously as she sought to escape a delight that was almost too much to bear.

'And this...' Simon demanded, his voice thicker, rawer. 'Is this the first time, too?'

She cried out as his mouth took her engorged flesh, too tormented to stop herself, her spine arching as her fingers clutched at his shoulders, wanting to prolong the agony that was his savagely sweet sucking of her breast and yet wanting to end it at the same time.

She sobbed his name; felt it torn from her throat as an expression of all that she was experiencing, and shuddered wildly beneath the slight grate of his teeth against her, as he slowly released her.

'Feel what you're doing to me, Jenna. See what touching you makes me feel,' he begged, roughly drawing her hand against his body to where it pulsed fiercely in masculine arousal.

'I want you. I want to make love to you, but not here…not like this.'

His words brought her back to her senses.

'No! No. We… You…'

You don't love me, she had been about to say, but she tensed suddenly as she heard his mother calling her name.

It was too late for them to do anything. Simon tugged her top into place, and protected her with the bulk of his body, but Jenna knew immediately from her embarrassment that his mother was well aware of what she had interrupted.

'Oh!' She faltered and looked uncertainly at them. 'Simon, I…Jenna, I know it's not your night, but I was wondering if you would cook dinner tonight. My tummy's still bothering me a bit…'

They took it in turns to prepare the meals, and Jenna nodded in quick agreement, knowing that her face still burned with embarrassed colour as Simon's mother turned and hurried away.

She bit her lip and waited for Simon to say something. Unlike her he seemed totally unconcerned, almost in some sense pleased. As though he was *glad* that his mother had seen them.

'I'd better go in.' She tried to get up, but his fingers circled her wrist, stopping her.

'Not yet, Jenna. We have to talk. My mother obviously now believes that we're lovers.'

'Yes.'

'This puts an entirely different complexion on our engagement, don't you agree? We can hardly break it off now.'

Jenna stared at him.

'What do you mean? We've got to, some time or another...and I suppose your mother must have assumed that we were lovers, anyway...'

'Assuming it is one thing. Being confronted with the reality of it is quite another,' Simon told her firmly.

'What are you saying?' She was thoroughly confused and slightly afraid.

'I'm suggesting that we bring this phony engagement to an end...'

Her relief was short-lived, as he added calmly, 'And make it a real one, followed by a real marriage...'

'But...but...but that's impossible,' she protested.

His mouth twisted. 'You're not very flattering, are you? Why should it be? Why shouldn't a marriage between us have just as much, if not more chance of success than any other?'

'Because we don't love each other.' She looked at him in bewilderment. 'Simon, you *can't* want to marry me.'

'Why not? I consider that we're highly compatible. We have similar backgrounds, similar views and interest, sexually...' He smiled mirthlessly as the colour flooded her face.

'But that isn't enough. There must be something more.'

'Like what?'

'Like...like love...emotion...' She spread her hands. 'Nobody marries simply because...'

'Look, why don't you think about it?' he interrupted firmly. 'OK, at the moment you're not in the right frame of mind to make any sort of decision, but I meant what I said, Jenna. I think a marriage between us would be a very good thing.'

But for whom? Jenna wondered bitterly later. What sort of marriage was Simon envisaging? One where he continued to have his life and loves in London while she remained discreetly tucked away in the country? Was that what he had in mind?

Oh, why was she even considering it? It was ridiculous, preposterous. Surely she wasn't such a pathetic fool that she hoped that if she did marry him he might eventually come to love her?

It seemed to Jenna that evening that dinner was a rather subdued affair, whether because she herself had so much on her mind, or because Susie and John had gone, or because Simon's mother was still bothered by the pain in her side, she didn't know.

While Simon made up a fourth at cards, she kept herself busy in the kitchen, knowing she was acting out of cowardice, but unable to stop herself.

Susie rang at nine o'clock to say that they had been lucky enough to make all their arrangements and that the wedding was to take place in exactly three weeks' time.

'John's parents will fly over,' she told Jenna when she spoke to her. 'And then we shall all fly back together. We're going to spend our honeymoon in a very quiet resort John knows, and his family want the parents to come over for Christmas. And that invite includes you and Simon and your grandmother as well, Jen.'

'Oh, I don't think—' Jenna began to demur, but Susie wouldn't let her.

'Please think seriously about coming. After this Christmas things will be different. John and I want to start a family as soon as possible... We've wasted too much time already.'

Hearing Susie—scatter-brained, feather-headed Susie—talking so seriously and earnestly about having children brought on a bitter wave of loneliness.

As teenagers, *she* had been the one who wanted a husband and a family...and now... And now she was desperately in love with a man who only wanted to marry her because she fitted into the slot in his mind he had entitled 'wife'.

It wasn't enough, and it would never be enough— not for her, and she had to tell him as much.

CHAPTER TEN

IT WAS easier said than done. Every time Jenna tried to intimate that she wanted to speak to Simon alone, he managed to avoid her—deliberately so, she was sure. Well, if he thought she would give in by default, he would soon learn he was wrong. There were a dozen or more excellent reasons why she shouldn't marry, but as far as she was concerned, the most important one of all was the one she could not divulge to him.

In less than a week they would all be going home, and what would happen then?

Since the afternoon when Simon had made love to her, she had avoided her old spot by the river. Simon's mother had all but got the wedding planned.

Six months ago, she would have said it was inconceivable that Simon would choose to marry and settle down, especially for such a mundane reason, but these last few weeks, viewing him from an adult stance rather than an adoring teenage one, she had come to see that he was a man to whom family and tradition mattered strongly.

They were having lunch with the Le Bruns, and

guessing that it would be a rather formal affair Jenna returned to the farmhouse to change.

She had just had a shower and was about to put on clean underwear when she heard the knock on her door. She went to open it, wrapping a towel round her still damp body.

For some reason she had expected to see her grandmother outside, but it was Simon, and he took advantage of her momentary surprise to walk past her and into her room.

'Simon, you can't come in here. What do you want?'

'You've been dropping broad hints that you want to talk to me for the last few days and now that I oblige, you want to know what I want?' His eyebrows rose mockingly as he challenged her to repudiate his statement.

'You know quite well why I wanted to talk to you... We've got to put an end to this engagement...'

She kept her back to him, hugging the towel more firmly round her body, wishing that he would go away, and yet conversely wanting him to stay.

When he made no response she turned round and looked at him.

'Has there really been no man in your life? No lover?' he said abruptly. 'When I see you like this I can't believe it...'

She could have told him that her childish infatuation with him hadn't left room for anyone else, but she restrained herself, suddenly aware of the intimacy and the danger of her situation.

'Maybe I'm just not very highly sexually motivated,' she responded lightly, trying to banish the tension enclosing them.

She realised instantly that it was the wrong thing to have said.

There was a look in his eyes as he came towards her that made excitement kick sharply through her body at exactly the same time as she shivered with fear.

'I could very easily prove that that's just not so, and take the greatest pleasure in doing so,' he said softly.

Instantly her body went weak with longing. 'No!'

'Jenna, we're leaving in ten minutes,' Simon's father called as he walked downstairs.

'Saved by the hand of fate,' Simon mocked her. 'But not for ever, Jenna...'

'I'm not going to marry you, Simon, and if you won't tell everyone, then I'll tell them myself.'

She felt better once she had said it, stronger.

'What is it you're afraid of? Marriage, or me?'

'Neither,' she told him as calmly as she could. 'It's simply that when I do marry I want to marry for love.'

She turned her back on him abruptly, hardly able to believe it when she heard her bedroom door open and close quietly behind him.

Now that he was gone she was shaking with reaction—and regret? Why on earth couldn't she be more pragmatic...more...more adult? Why couldn't she take what he was offering and be happy with it?

Quite simply because she was not that sort of person. Had she been, she would have forgotten her teenage infatuation with Simon much earlier, supplanted it with someone else...

She found the silk suit she was looking for at the back of her wardrobe and pulled it on hurriedly.

She had bought it the previous year in the sale at Harvey Nichols, and it was strikingly different from anything else she had in her wardrobe; a short, straight, deep yellow silk skirt topped with a subtly subdued 'Dynasty' style jacket in a vivid array of colours on the same deep yellow background as the skirt.

She swept her hair back off her face, securing it with a pair of antique combs she had found in a small antique shop, and made up her face discreetly.

She arrived downstairs just ahead of Simon. Like herself he was dressed formally, and it came as a shock to see him thus attired after the casual wear of jeans and shirt he had been wearing for the last few weeks.

It took her back to the night he had arrived at her flat looking for Susie.

'Simon, when are you going to get Jenna an engagement ring?' his mother enquired. 'Susie rang this morning to say that John had bought her the most beautiful star sapphire.'

'Jenna's will be ready when we get back to London. I've had it specially designed.'

Jenna looked suspiciously at him. Was he lying? She sincerely hoped so, because if he wasn't he was going to have wasted his money.

They set out for the Le Bruns in both cars. Jenna tried to suggest that Simon take his mother as his passenger, but she demurred.

'Simon's car's far too racy and uncomfortable for me. You go with him.'

The Le Bruns had several other guests for lunch, all of them extremely elegantly dressed. Simon and Jenna were introduced to them as a couple, and it was frightening to Jenna how much she enjoyed being paired with him.

But not for much longer. She was determined that just as soon as this holiday was over the engagement was going to be broken, even if she had to write herself to Simon's parents to tell them.

Perhaps it was cowardly of her to break the news by letter, but then it was not through her doing that the 'engagement' had come into being in the first place.

Jenna already knew that the French treated lunch as their most important meal of the day. At precisely twelve-thirty, Madame Le Brun ushered them all into her elegant dining-room. Crystal and silver glittered on the highly polished table with its centrepiece of flowers.

French windows were open to the light breeze.

Jenna was not seated with Simon, but with the son of the local doctor and his wife, who had just returned from Africa where he had been working for one of the famine relief agencies. A tall, almost painfully thin man with a shock of curly hair, he had spoken passionately before lunch of the work the agencies were doing.

He had an almost missionary zeal about him, a commitment to his work that no one could doubt.

Madame Le Brun had whispered to Jenna in an aside that he had been sent home because of his own health, which had suffered in the months he had been working in the famine relief camps.

Despite his almost monastic air he was still very much a Frenchman, instinctively gallant and complimentary, Jenna noticed with amusement, although in Jenna's case his compliments were reserved not for her person, but for her interest and knowledge in his work.

'In Paris they give lunches and balls to raise money for the hungry, but the talk is all of the latest affair, or the latest government scandal...' He shrugged bitterly. 'They cannot conceive what it is like to be so hungry and weak that to take the merest sip of milk is a feat to compare with climbing Everest. And yet they walk for mile after mile to come to us...mothers with children...sisters with brothers. It is the tragedy of our time, a scourge as bestial as any medieval disease...'

Jenna let him talk, sensing that he needed an outlet for the anger all dammed up inside him.

Every now and again she was conscious of Simon watching her, but whenever she glanced in his direction he seemed deep in conversation with his partner, a woman in her late forties, who had been introduced to them as Monsieur Le Brun's widowed sister-in-law.

To start the meal they had been served with Tourin Périgourdine, a vegetable soup that was a specialty of the region, and, as small helpings of pâté de foie gras embellished with *cèpes*, the fine delicate mushrooms of the Dordogne, were put before them, Jean glanced at his with a faint grimace of distaste.

'I am a Frenchman,' he said to Jenna, 'and yet when I know that my countrymen allow the goose who provides this delicacy for us to eat until its size is completely distorted, and consider themselves epicureans for doing so, while all the time their fellow human beings are starving, I wonder at the wisdom of what we are pleased to call civilisation.'

Jenna sympathised with him, but she suspected from the look his mother had just given him that she had overheard his comment and disapproved of it, especially when voiced at someone else's table.

She agreed diplomatically with what he had said, and then gently tried to change the subject. Jean was somewhere about her own age, but he looked older—older in some ways than Simon.

A main course followed the pâté—lamb with accompanying vegetables and a special sauce—and then a fresh, delicate sorbet.

Jenna had refused any dessert, and when Jean suggested a walk round the Le Bruns' extensive gardens, to offset the effects of their lunch, she agreed.

She glimpsed Simon frowning slightly as they walked outside, but reminded herself of exactly what the realities of their situation were. He didn't love her and he never would. He wanted to marry her simply because he thought they got on well enough together. That might be enough for him, but it wasn't enough for her.

Although she listened dutifully to all that Jean told her about his work as they toured the gardens, her attention was only peripheral. Deep down inside she was thinking about Simon...thinking about life without him...

When she heard him call her name it startled her. He was hurrying towards them, down the long *allée* of poplar trees, and her heart leaped with pleasure as, just for a moment, she allowed herself to think that the anxiety in his voice and face was for her.

She was soon disillusioned.

'It's Ma,' he told her abruptly. 'She's not well. The Le Bruns offered to call their doctor, but I think it would be better if we drove her straight to the nearest hospital...'

'What...?'

'I think it might be appendicitis. Apparently she's been having pains on and off for some time, but hasn't done anything about it. It's only this last few days that they've become more acute.

'Pa will drive her there and your grandmother will go with them, since she speaks good French. I offered to go, but your grandmother suggested that we go back to the farmhouse and wait there for news. It makes sense, really. We'd only be in the way at the hospital.'

As he spoke he was hurrying back to the house, and Jenna almost had to run to keep up with him.

When they got there they found that his father had already left. The Le Bruns were very anxious and concerned, but once Simon had assured them that they would be in touch the moment they had any news, they were allowed to leave.

'I'm sure she'll be all right.'

Instinctively she reached out to touch him in a gesture of both compassion and reassurance. His grip on her fingers as he looked at her made her wonder how on earth she had ever thought him invulnerable and removed from all real human emotion.

They didn't speak on the drive back to the cottage, and the first thing Simon did once they were inside was to ring the hospital.

The news was reassuring. It *was* appendicitis, his father told Simon, but thankfully it had been caught in good time.

'They're going to operate this afternoon. Harriet and I have booked into a small hotel here, and we'll be staying the night, just in case we're needed. Harriet has just gone out to buy your mother a nightdress and one or two things. Don't worry, we'll ring you just as soon as the operation's over.'

Simon was holding the receiver so that Jenna could hear what was being said.

After having confirmed that his mother was not in any immediate danger, he told his father that they would stay at the farmhouse until they heard from him again.

Somehow as he replaced the receiver, his right arm slipped round Jenna's shoulders, holding her against him.

Sensing his need, she didn't move away, knowing instinctively that the comforting intimacy of their body contact was something he needed.

'You heard everything?'

Jenna nodded her head, moving away from him. 'Yes. I'm sure she'll be all right...'

'I'd better ring Susie and let her know.'

He sounded preoccupied, almost distant, their earlier shared concern banished, leaving Jenna feeling almost deserted.

'I suppose I ought to go upstairs and make a start on the packing—your parents will probably want to go straight home from the hospital, and we would have been leaving anyway in a few days...'

Simon nodded, but Jenna felt that his mind was elsewhere. He was probably worrying about breaking the news to Susie in a way that would not have her rushing over to France on the first available flight.

JENNA DID HER own packing first, leaving out just enough things to get her through the few remaining days, and then she did her grandmother's.

Both her grandmother and Simon's father would need a change of clothes if they were staying in a hotel overnight, a fact which she felt she ought to mention to Simon.

He was standing staring out of the sitting-room window when she went down.

He frowned as he listened to her.

'Yes. You're right. Could you pack a few things for them? I'll drive to the hospital and leave them there.'

It didn't take her long, and although she knew it was only sensible that one of them remained behind to take any phone calls, nevertheless Jenna felt very alone as she watched him drive away.

By the time he came back, she had answered a concerned telephone call from the Le Bruns, and almost completed all the packing. She had just started to clean out the kitchen cupboards when she heard his car.

He looked a little happier than he had done when he left, but he was still frowning, and she couldn't help but notice how he stepped back from her as though avoiding her touch when she went to the door to let him in.

'How's your mother?' she asked, ignoring the pain caused by his withdrawal.

'In the operating theatre. There aren't any complications, and as Pa said they caught it just in time. Your grandmother is masterminding everything for him; the fact that she speaks such good French has made it all a lot easier... They're going to stay on to be near the hospital for a couple of days, and then they're going to make arrangements to go straight home from there. Dad said to leave the keys and their luggage, and they'll pick them up on the way...'

'Leave them?' Jenna was confused. Surely *they* would be staying in France until his parents were ready to go back as they had originally planned?

'There isn't much point in us staying on,' Simon told her flatly, avoiding looking at her. 'I'll ring up tonight and see if we can change our ferry booking. We might as well leave first thing in the morning, I think...' Something had happened, changed. It was almost as though he couldn't bear to be with her. Ridiculously, it hurt.

'All the packing's done, apart from yours... I thought we'd have a light meal, omelette and salad, something like that...'

'That sounds fine.' He was almost curt with her—the Simon she remembered from their past encounters.

All of a sudden, Jenna wanted to put as much distance between them as possible.

'I think I'll go out for a walk,' she said stiffly.

Simon made no comment. What had she been expecting? That he would stop her? Demand that she stay with him?

Angrily she hurried towards the footpath that led to the village.

SHE WAS GONE much longer than she had anticipated, and in the end it was only hunger that drove her back, her footsteps slowing as she approached the farmhouse.

It was only when she saw that Simon's car was still parked outside that she acknowledged that she had half expected it not to be there. He had made it so plain that he didn't want her company that it was almost a shock to discover he was still here.

She walked into the kitchen and saw that it was immaculately clean. Had he made himself something to eat? She opened the fridge in a mood of angry unhappiness, reaching for the eggs. Well, if he didn't want her company she wouldn't inflict it on him. She would eat by herself.

She slammed the door viciously, and as she turned round Simon walked through from the sitting-room.

'You're back.'

'That's right,' she agreed bitingly. 'But don't worry, I'm not going to inflict myself on you...'

He came towards her. 'Jenna...'

With a shock she recognised the smell of whisky on his breath. 'You've been drinking! Why?'

He laughed harshly, stepping away from her to lean against the door-frame.

'You might well ask! To keep me out of your bed, Jenna, that's why,' he told her brutally. 'And I intend to go on drinking to the point where I can lose my eyes, and sleep without torturing myself with impossible images of you there beside me.' He saw her face and laughed again. 'You don't have the faintest idea what I'm talking about, do you?' He left the door, straightening up and coming towards her so fast that she couldn't avoid him, his hands grasping her arms as he said thickly, 'I want you…I want you so much that there's no way I could stay in this house with you tonight and not make love to you…'

'No… No, I don't believe you! You're making it up,' Jenna protested wildly.

'Am I?'

Just the way he said it made tremors of reaction spread wildly through her body.

'Jenna.'

Her breath caught in her throat as he said her name in something between a groan and a protest, reaching hungrily for her, his mouth against her own demanding that she acknowledge his desire.

After his earlier coolness, it was too much to resist. She felt herself almost melting into him, responding to him in such a way that it was hardly surprising that he should pick her up and carry her through the emptiness of the farmhouse to the privacy of his bedroom.

She knew she ought to protest, to stop this insanity before it went any further, but how could she when her heart and her body cried out yearningly for him?

'Jenna…Jenna…'

The sound of her name whispered between kisses of frantic passion assaulted her senses like the most effective of love potions.

Her clothes seemed to slide from her body, leaving her free to press herself fiercely against him.

She heard him groan and didn't even realise it was because she was touching him until he wrenched free of his shirt and pressed both her hands flat to his torso and imprisoned them there, while his mouth ravished the sensitive tips of her breasts.

His need, his wanting were now hers, and she went willingly, eagerly where he led, shuddering in delight when at last she felt the primitive naked heat of his body pressing her into the softness of the bed.

She wanted him. Needed him so much that she couldn't live another second without his possession. Her fingertips found the curve of his spine and followed it downwards to the lean hardness of his buttocks.

'Oh God, Jenna.'

His spine arched, his hips thrusting anguishedly against her, a harsh moan of need and deprivation shuddering against her skin.

Instinctively her fingers clenched, her nails digging wantonly into his flesh.

Now that it was almost here, this moment of oneness and communion she had never shared with anyone else, there was a rightness, a certainty about it that left no room for doubts or fears.

Her body arched compliantly, eager for his. She felt him hesitate and she cried his name achingly.

His hands moved down her body, supporting her, lifting her against him and she shuddered beneath the first probing thrust of him.

It was almost shocking, how eagerly her flesh adapted to him, wanting him...cocooning him, welcoming each powerful movement of him within her that took her higher and higher into the realms of delight.

Helpless beneath the storm of sensations sweeping her, she clung to him, shuddering uncontrollably with the desire building inside her.

She heard him cry out, and felt the explosive force of his body's release, and only registered what it meant in terms of her own curtailed pleasure slowly as she felt him withdraw from her.

Deprivation swept through her. She heard Simon say something and swallowed hard, striving to control her own tautly strung need. He moved, and she shuddered visibly as his hand touched her body intimately.

She wanted his touch so much, and yet it was surely wrong that he should be doing this to her?

She must have said something without realising it, because she heard him whisper rawly, 'No, no, it's my fault. I couldn't wait... Let me do this for you, Jenna... Let me show you how it can be...'

And then incredibly she felt his mouth moving against her with delicate intimacy, conjuring up such

a storm of feelings that she couldn't even cry out her
shock. His tongue stroked, cajoled and pleasured her
until the tiny flutters of sensation deep inside her
grew and spread, and then, surely impossibly, he was
entering her again, and she could taste the feminine
scent of her own body on his mouth.

This time it was different…this time her body
broke into wave after wave of exquisite sensation
that made her cry out in wonder.

She lay wrapped in his arms for a long time afterwards, caught somewhere between fantasy and reality, reluctant to destroy the perfection of what had
been.

It was Simon who broke the silence first, rolling
over and cupping her face, his eyes and voice sombre
as he said softly, 'God, Jenna, I'm sorry.'

'Don't be…' How odd that she should be the one
to comfort him, her fingers automatically smoothing
through the disordered thickness of her hair as he
pillowed his head between her breasts. 'I wanted
what happened just as much as you,' she admitted
huskily.

He lifted his head and grimaced ironically. 'I don't
think so… You see, I don't just want your body…I
want you heart, your soul, I want *you*, Jenna. I love
you and its tearing me apart… I promised myself I'd
never tell you…never burden you with it…'

She looked at him, trying to find something in his
expression that would tell her that he was lying, that

this was all some sort of game, but there was nothing there to see but anguish and remorse.

'I've loved you for years. All those years when you've avoided and disliked me, and I've wanted you for even longer.' His fingertips traced the outline of her mouth. 'I want you now,' he told her softly, his eyes darkening as he saw the responsive flush of colour stain her skin.

'But you can't, we've...'

'I know...' He cut through her whispered protest with a grim smile. 'It should be impossible...'

'Is...is that why you wanted to marry me... because you love me?' Jenna asked, looking directly at him for the first time.

'Yes... God, I thought all my prayers were answered when Mrs M rang Ma and gave her the news that we were engaged. All I needed was another miracle to make our engagement real instead of fake and I was home and dry, and when Ma discovered us on the verge of making love, I thought I'd got it. But I realised today when I watched you with Jean that I can't force my love on you, can't make you love me in return...'

Jenna felt as though she was going to cry. It was disconcerting to see Simon so humbled.

'I...'

'Don't say anything,' he told her, 'but promise me one thing, Jen. If...if there should be any repercussions from...from today, you'll tell me, won't you?'

She stared at him and then realised what he meant.

'Is that why you made love to me? Because you hoped I might get pregnant?'

He laughed harshly.

'No, even I'm not that Machiavellian. I made love to you purely and simply because I want and love you so much that I couldn't stop myself. You know you're the first woman who has ever made me feel like that. The first and the last. There's nothing I'd like more than to see your body growing with my child,' he told her thickly, shifting so that he could cover her stomach with his hand. 'I'm selfish enough to want it to be...to want you to have conceived my child, because I know that if you have you will marry me... You're not cut out for single motherhood, and I know you well enough to know you'd never have an abortion. But I hope I've retained enough sanity to know that nothing good could come out of such a forced marriage—not for you, not for me, and not for our child... If you ever come to me I want it to be freely, even if it has to be without love...'

Jenna could hardly speak for the lump in her throat. 'Simon...'

She reached out to touch him but he moved away, saying firmly, 'No, Jenna. I don't want your pity. I know what a soft heart you've got.' He cupped her face and looked seriously at her. 'I also understand that what happened now between us was, for you, something that was left over from the past. Call it a tying up of loose ends... No, don't look away from me. You haven't done anything you need to feel guilty about.' She felt his chest expand as he breathed in steadyingly. 'I feel...privileged that you should have chosen me as your first lover, but I know that emotionally I have no claims on you.'

The phone rang abruptly and imperatively before Jenna could contradict him.

'I'll get it—it will be the hospital...'

Jenna watched him as he pulled on his robe, flushing slightly as she caught sight of the marks she herself had inflicted.

He was gone for quite a long time. Long enough for her to get dressed, she realised suddenly. No doubt he thought he was being tactful. Doubt suddenly struck her—what if what he had just said about loving her had been simply a palliative, simply the words he always used to escape from a commitment he didn't want. But no, there had been no mistaking the emotion in his voice or his eyes. She might not be experienced sexually where men were concerned, but she doubted that what she had just shared with Simon could have been born of anything other than a very deep need.

Resolutely she went back to her own room and pulled on her own robe.

She found Simon in the kitchen making coffee.

'I thought you might welcome a cup,' he told her without turning round.

'Was it the hospital on the phone?'

'Yes. The operation's over successfully—we can

go and visit tomorrow if we like.' He turned towards her. 'Jenna—'

'No, please don't say anything yet,' she interrupted him. 'There's something I have to say first.' She swallowed hard. 'When you—when you said that we should get married, and I refused, it was because...because...' She forced herself to look directly at him, still half expecting to see rejection in his eyes. 'It was because I thought you didn't love me,' she told him in a slightly wobbly voice, finishing in a rush, 'and I couldn't bear that...not when I love you so much...'

The silence seemed to stretch into eternity. She closed her eyes, not wanting to see his face. She heard him move and thought for a moment he had left the kitchen, and then when she opened them again she found that he had moved quickly and silently towards her.

'My God, Jen! Say it again...'

'Which bit?'

He shook her.

'You know which bit, damn you! Am I hearing things, or did I just hear you saying that you love me?'

There was such a male note of satisfaction and relief in his voice that she almost laughed. *This* was the Simon she knew—assured, in control.

'Stop tormenting me,' he groaned, the satisfaction suddenly gone. 'Let me hear you say it again.'

She liked this vulnerability in him—all the more

so because she knew it was a facet of his personality that would only be revealed to her. It was his love for her that made him vulnerable... In the same way that she was vulnerable to him.

'I love you, Simon.'

She sighed blissfully as she was silenced by the intoxicating heat of his mouth as it moved possessively over hers...

It seemed a long time before he released her.

'I'd better ring Susie and let her know that Ma's OK...'

'Yes, speaking of which,' Jenna said drily, 'surely you didn't honestly think that John would switch his affections from Susie to me?'

'No, I knew how he felt about her, but it was you I was dubious about... I thought you might be in danger of falling for him.'

'So you rang Susie and persuaded her to come over here, by telling her that John was in danger of being stolen away by her supposed best friend...'

He groaned remorsefully. 'I was going insane with jealousy. All this time I've waited for you to notice me, to stop looking at me as though I was the lowest form of human life, and when I get the opportunity to show you how it could be between us, along comes John, stealing you away from me...'

'I had to convince myself I didn't like you,' Jenna told him simply. 'Otherwise I think I would simply have fallen apart. All those elegant ladies who have passed through your life, Simon.'

'Passed through being the operative phrase,' he said firmly 'You will marry me, won't you, Jen?'

He laughed triumphantly when he saw the look in her eyes, and whispered in her ear, 'I'm almost beginning to think it was worth all the wait and the agony you've put me through just to see that look in your eyes.'

THREE WEEKS later on the lawn of the Townsends' Gloucestershire house, Jenna stood next to Susie and John, congratulating them on their marriage earlier that day. The flowers in the garden vied with the outfits of the female wedding guests and the sun shone from a perfectly blue summer's sky.

'Ma tells me that you still haven't sorted out who you're going to have as a page boy,' Susie told Jenna, grinning at her brother as she did so.

Jenna gave him a mischievous smile and said *sotto voce*, 'Oh yes, we have, we're having them both...'

Simon groaned, and Jenna laughed up at him, teasing, 'We could always get married in a register office.'

He looked at her for a long time, and then, as though they were completely alone, he said softly, 'No, I've waited so long for you that I want to tie you to me with every law that man and God have devised. I want everyone to know that you're mine.'

He lifted her hand to his mouth and gently placed a kiss in her palm.

'Look at them,' Susie said wryly to her mother.

'Why do they make me feel as though somehow I've missed out on something?'

'You could never live with a man like Simon,' her mother told her. 'You'd find him far too possessive and demanding. John loves you and you love him.'

'Yes,' Susie agreed, looking towards the group of people around her new husband, and adding with a cheery grin, 'But I wouldn't mind betting for all that we got married first, Simon and Jen will be the first to present you with a grandchild—and it will be a son, knowing my brother.'

She looked without rancour to where Simon and Jen stood together, isolated from the rest of the guests.

'Have I told you today how much I love you?' Simon murmured, bending his head so that his lips just brushed the delicate skin beneath Jenna's ear.

She shivered deliciously.

'Yes...yes, I think you have.'

'Pity,' he said reluctantly. 'I was about to offer to show you instead... How long is it now before you're legally mine?'

'Another four weeks.'

He groaned. 'Far too long...far, far too long. Once you *are* mine, Jenna, I'm never going to let you go,' he told her, suddenly serious.

She met his look frankly and openly. 'I'll never want you to. I love you now and I always will. Always...'

'As I love you.' He bent his head and kissed her,

and a mischievous young second cousin took the opportunity to snap them with his new camera, which was how he came to present them with the printed result in a very elegant art deco silver frame as a wedding present almost a month to the day later.

Harlequin Romance®

Delightful

Affectionate

Romantic

Emotional

Tender

Original

Daring

Riveting

Enchanting

Adventurous

Moving

Harlequin Romance—the
series that has it all!

HROM-G

HARLEQUIN PRESENTS®

The world's bestselling romance series...
The series that brings you your favorite authors,
month after month:

Helen Bianchin...Emma Darcy
Lynne Graham...Penny Jordan
Miranda Lee...Sandra Morton
Anne Mather...Carole Mortimer
Susan Napier...Michelle Reid

and many more uniquely talented authors!

Wealthy, powerful, gorgeous men...
Women who have feelings just like your own...
The stories you love, set in exotic, glamorous locations...

HARLEQUIN PRESENTS,
Seduction and passion guaranteed!

Harlequin® Historical

From rugged lawmen and
valiant knights to defiant heiresses
and spirited frontierswomen,
Harlequin Historicals will
capture your imagination with
their dramatic scope, passion
and adventure.

Harlequin Historicals...
they're too good to miss!

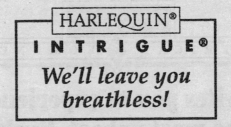

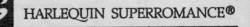

HARLEQUIN SUPERROMANCE®

...there's more to the story!

Superromance. A *big* satisfying read about unforget-
table characters. Each month we offer
four very different stories that range from family
drama to adventure and mystery, from highly emotional stories to romantic comedies—and
much more! Stories about people you'll
believe in and care about. Stories too
compelling to put down....

Our authors are among today's *best* romance writ-
ers. You'll find familiar names and
talented newcomers. Many of them are
award winners—and you'll see why!

If you want the biggest and best
in romance fiction, you'll get it
from Superromance!

Available wherever Harlequin books are sold.

HARLEQUIN®
Makes any time special.™

Upbeat, all-American romances about the pursuit of love, marriage and family.

❖ HARLEQUIN®
Duets™
Two brand-new, full-length romantic comedy novels for one low price.

Rich and vivid historical romances that capture the imagination with their dramatic scope, passion and adventure.

❖HARLEQUIN®
Temptation
Sexy, sassy and seductive— Temptation is hot sizzling romance.

❖ HARLEQUIN®
SUPERROMANCE
A bigger romance read with more plot, more story-line variety, more pages and a romance that's evocatively explored.

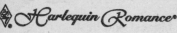
Love stories that capture the essence of traditional romance.

HARLEQUIN®
INTRIGUE®
Dynamic mysteries with a thrilling combination of breathtaking romance and heart-stopping suspense.

Meet sophisticated men of the world and captivating women in glamorous, international settings.